THE KNIGHT AND DEATH

and

ONE WAY OR ANOTHER

LEONARDO SCIASCIA was born in Sicily in 1912. He was a renowned Italian novelist and essayist, as well as a polemical and outspoken political commentator who, like many of the protagonists in his novels, challenged the entrenched corruption in the government of his day. He has been described by Gore Vidal as one of the greatest modern writers. He died in 1989.

THE KNIGHT AND DEATH

and

ONE WAY OR ANOTHER

Leonardo Sciascia

Translated from the Italian by

JOSEPH FARRELL
AND SACHA RABINOVITCH

GRANTA

Granta Publications, 12 Addison Avenue, London W11 4QR

First published in Great Britain by Granta Books 2003
This edition published by Granta Books 2013
First published in Italian as *Il Cavaliere e la Morte*, 1988
and *Todo Modo*, 1974

Copyright © Leonardo Sciascia Estate
Handled by Agenzia Letteraria Internazionale, Milan, Italy
Published in Italy by Adelphi Edizioni, Milan

Translation copyright © Joseph Farrell, 1991
and Sacha Rabinovitch, 1987

A CIP catalogue record for this book is available
from the British Library.

1 3 5 7 9 10 8 6 4 2

ISBN 978 1 84708 930 4

Printed and bound by CPI Group (UK) Ltd, Croydon, CR0 4YY

Contents

THE KNIGHT AND DEATH

(a *sotie*)

Translated by Joseph Farrell

An old Danish bishop, I remember, once told me that there are many ways of reaching truth, and that burgundy is one of the many.

Karen Blixen, *Seven Gothic Tales*

Each time he raised his eyes from the paper work, and even more each time he leaned his head against the top of the high, unyielding chair-back, he saw every detail, every outline in all its clarity, as though his gaze had newly acquired a subtlety and a sharpness, or as though the print were being reborn before his eyes with the same meticulous precision with which, in the year 1513, Albrecht Dürer had first engraved it. He had purchased it many years previously at an auction sale: one of those sudden, rash cravings for possession which, at certain times, in the presence of a painting, an etching or a book, took hold of him. He had competed for it with others who had themselves set their hearts on it, reaching a state of near hatred for the most tenacious of his rivals, who then casually abandoned it to him. The price corresponded to two months' salary, and when he came to handing over the money, the sum involved took him aback. At the time it was sizeable, and not only in relation to his ability to pay, but now, with the soaring rise of inflation and the tenfold increase in the value of the works of Dürer and all the other great engravers, it seemed derisory. He had taken it with him from one workplace to another, from one office to another, always choosing to hang it on the wall facing his desk, but of all those who, over the years, had passed through his office, only one (a talented swindler, who genially accepted the destiny which would see him taken from that office to become guest of some inhospitable prison for a period of years) had taken the time to look at it and appreciate it: to appreciate it fully, in the light of the most up-to-date catalogues of the print dealers of Paris and Zurich.

This appreciation had alarmed him somewhat; in an initial impulse of meanness or avarice he had decided to take it home, but the decision was forgotten almost as soon as it was made. He had long grown accustomed to having it there before him, in the many hours he spent in his office. *The Knight, Death and the Devil*. On the back, on the protecting cover, there were the titles, written in pencil in German and French: *Ritter, Tod und Teufel; Le Chevalier, la Mort et le Diable*. And mysteriously: *Christ? Savonarole?* Had the collector or dealer who had wondered about those two names perhaps thought that Dürer had wished to symbolize one or the other in the figure of the Knight?

Time and again, gazing at the print, he had asked himself that question. But now, leaning back in the chair in exhaustion and pain, he stared at it, groping for some meaning in that purchase made all those years ago. Death; and that castle in the background, unattainable.

With the many cigarettes he had smoked during the night, the ever-present pain had lost its heaviness and density, changing shade to a more diffuse agony. It was undoubtedly possible to give the names of colours to the different qualities and shifts of pain. At the moment it had changed from violet to red: flame red, in probing tongues which quite unpredictably pierced every part of his body, to linger there or fade away.

Automatically, he lit another cigarette, but would have let it burn out in the ashtray had not the Chief, on entering, launched into his customary tirade against the destructive habit of heavy smoking. A senseless vice, a death vice. He, the Chief, had given up smoking within the last six months, and was extremely proud of himself, but he still experienced, together with a certain pain, pangs of envy and rancour when he saw others smoke; both were nourished by the fact that, at the very time when the memory of smoking was to him like a paradise lost, the smell of smoke occasioned a discomfort which came close to nausea.

'Don't you feel suffocated in here?' said the Chief.

The Deputy picked up the cigarette from the ashtray and inhaled slowly and voluptuously. It was perfectly true. The atmosphere was suffocating. The room was full of smoke which hung thickly around the still burning lights; like a transparent curtain, it veiled the glass of the windows through which, flickeringly, morning was beginning to shine. He inhaled once more.

'I can understand,' said the Chief in a tone of superior tolerance, 'that certain people may lack the will power to kick the habit entirely, but to pursue a death of this kind with such stubbornness and self-indulgence … My brother-in-law …' He employed his brother-in-law, a chain-smoker deceased a few months previously, as a blind, in a delicate effort to avoid having to refer directly to the illness of which, plainly, the Deputy was intent on dying.

'I know. We were friends … You, I imagine, will have already chosen your own style of death. I must get you to talk to me about it one of these days. Who knows, you might even persuade me to choose it too.'

'I haven't chosen it, and it is not a thing that can be chosen; but now that I have given up smoking, I hope to die a different death.'

'You are no doubt aware it was the converted Jews who invented the Catholic Inquisition in Spain.'

He was not aware. And so: 'I have never had much time for the Jews, strictly between you and me.'

'I know, but I would have expected you to have some interest in converts.' They were almost colleagues, having known each other for years, and so could indulge, but always without malice, in the occasional ironic, pointed or even sarcastic remark. The Chief let them pass on account of the unease occasioned by the incomprehensible loyalty of the Deputy towards him. Never had he met a Deputy of such loyalty; initially he had left no stone unturned in his efforts to locate a hidden reason; now he knew there was none.

'Converts or not, I've no time for them. You, on the other hand ...'

'I, on the other hand have no time for converts, Jewish or not: every convert opts for something worse, even when it seems better. The worst, in someone who is capable of conversion, always becomes the very worst of the worst.'

'Conversion to not smoking has nothing to do with it: granted that conversion is generally an abomination.'

'It has everything to do with it: because the tendency is to become persecutors of those who still smoke.'

'How can you say that? Persecutors! If I were a persecutor, these offices would be filled with huge notices screaming No Smoking at you: it might be an idea – in spite of you, and for your own good. Because I am saying this for your good: my brother-in law ...'

'I know.'

'So, let's say no more about it. As regards your philosophy on converts, I could produce arguments to annihilate you, just like that.' The snap of the thumb and index fingers indicated the lightning speed of the act of annihilation. It was a gesture he employed frequently, because there was no limit to the number of things he planned to annihilate; and the Deputy, who sometimes attempted to imitate it, but without ever managing to produce the slightest snap, was prone to a childish envy on this account. 'However, we have work to do. Come with me.'

'Where?'

'You know already. Let's go.'

'Isn't it a bit early?'

'No, it's already seven o'clock: I was deliberately killing time with your philosophy.'

'Early, always early.' He hated the police custom of executing warrants, carrying out house searches, routine investigations and door-to-door enquiries in the early hours of the morning or, more often than not, at the dead of night. Both fellow officers and the lower ranks considered it a pleasure to be savoured whenever the slightest opportunity or the remotest justification presented itself. The thunderous knock at the door behind which unwitting families were enjoying their rest, their sleep; at the very hour when sleep, once the weight of exhaustion has been lightened, becomes less dark, more open to dreams, more blissful; the terrified – Who's there? and the solemn, booming reply – Police; the door held barely ajar, the eyes, distrustful and sleep-filled, peering out; the violent shove at the door, the rush of bodies; and inside, the agitated awakening of the whole family, the voices of fear and bewilderment, the crying of the children ... For such a delight, there was not a man in the force, whatever his rank, who would think twice about his own lost sleep. The Deputy, however, loved to sleep, after at least an hour with a book, right through from midnight to seven o'clock, and on the rare occasions when – invariably because of the division to which he was attached – he had to take part in such operations, he was always tormented by a personal sense of anguished shame.

'It's seven o'clock,' said the Chief, 'and it takes at least half an hour to get to Villaserena. After all, in the circumstances, I can hardly allow myself any special consideration, not even for him.'

'We have already allowed ourselves just that,' said the Deputy ironically. 'If it had been anyone else, we would have been there three hours ago, and already had the house upside down.'

'No doubt,' said the Chief, stung to the point of cynicism.

The black car waited for them in the courtyard – a beautiful, harmoniously colonnaded, baroque courtyard. There was no need to tell the policeman at the wheel where they were making for: everyone in the building which, buzzing as busily as any beehive, was even then coming back to life, was fully aware. How many calls, wondered the Deputy, had already gone out from that building to alert the President of the visit he was about to receive? The President: there was not the slightest need to add 'of United Industries', because in that city, anyone referring to 'the President' without further qualification had only one person in mind; for any other President, not excluding the President of the Republic, some specification was essential.

They remained silent for the entire half hour of the drive, or race, in the traffic which grew more frantic by the minute. The Chief cast and considered, recast and reconsidered what he would say to the President: concern was written on his face like the toothache. The Deputy knew him well enough to be able to decipher every detail of that concern: almost word for word; with each and every erasure, correction and replacement that he judged suitable for the case. A palimpsest.

They arrived at the villa. The officer at the wheel (I have been overcome by a sudden inhibition about using the word *driver:* with a sense of regret at having used it on other occasions; but will it ever again be possible to say, as was common in my childhood, *chauffeur?*) got out and rang the bell at the gatehouse long and imperiously. The Chief's toothache gave him a visible, stabbing pain: not like that, for God's sake! There are ways and ways. But he said nothing, out of deference to custom.

The Chief gave only his own name to the doorman who came forward. Not to mention the word Police seemed to him the first act of consideration due to the President: but the doorman was sufficiently quick-witted and experienced to grasp that he should announce – two gentlemen from the police, even if, as a Southerner, the word 'gentlemen' stuck in his craw; he made up for it with the contempt he put into the pronunciation. He came back without saying a word: he opened the gate and signed to them to proceed along the avenue towards the villa which could be seen at the foot of the tree-lined driveway, in all its enchantment, in all its song. ('When a building sings, it is architecture.')

Everything – entrance hall, staircases, corridors, library and President's studio – of a fragile, musical rococo, as though indeed a burst of song.

They had not long to wait: the President glided in silently from behind a curtain. He was clad in a velvet dressing-gown, but was already shaved and on the point of dressing with that severe and sure elegance which the fashion journals – now of each and every fashion – attributed to him. There hovered in the air around him an irritation at being compelled to delay his customary, almost lengendarily punctual, morning departure for the offices of United Industries, from whose top floor, as though in confidential familiarity with heaven, he took the daily, invariably correct, decisions which kept the whole country on the road to affluence and well-being; even if it was besieged on one side by the spectre of poverty, and on the other by that of plague.

'To what do I owe the pleasure of this unaccustomed visit?' asked the President, taking his time over shaking the Chief's hand and almost ignoring the Deputy's. He uttered the word 'unaccustomed' as though watching it materialise in large italics.

The Chief spluttered, as everything he had prepared fled from his mind, like hydrogen from a punctured balloon. He said: 'You knew Sandoz, the lawyer, well and ...'

'We are friends,' replied the President, 'but as to knowing him well ... you don't even know your own children well ... in fact, you invariably know them badly, very badly indeed. In other words, Signor Sandoz is a friend of mine, we see each other a lot, we have interests which are, if not exactly in common, at least closely related. But you said, I think, *knew*: so ...'

The Chief and the Deputy exchanged understanding glances. There flitted into those minds trained in distrust and suspicion, trained in the setting of word traps or in picking up stray words which could be converted into traps, the certainty that the President already knew – and it hardly came as a surprise, since there was no shortage of his acolytes in their offices – of the death of Sandoz. The Chief immediately put the thought aside, in the belief that for his part the President had a mind trained in not compromising his informers. He said: 'Unfortunately, Signor Sandoz is no more: he was murdered this evening, probably some time after midnight.'

'Murdered?'

'Murdered.'

'Unbelievable! I left him just shortly before midnight. We said goodbye at the door of the La Vecchia Cucina restaurant ... Murdered! But why? And by whom?'

'If we knew, we would not be here taking up your time.'

'Unbelievable!' repeated the President, but then he corrected himself. 'Unbelievable! ... what am I saying? Nowadays in this country everything is believable, everything is possible ... I myself ...' He was unable to make up his mind, thought the Deputy, between pretending he wanted to show them out and admitting that he understood there was more to come and that he had other questions to answer. By placing his hands on the arms of the chair as though to raise himself and see them to the door, he chose the pretence; ill-advisedly because the Chief sensed it instinctively and, quite unconsciously, freed himself of the unease to which he had been prey until that moment. As was normal when beginning an interrogation, he settled into the armchair as though taking up residence in it. His voice trembled with the customary – *Say what you please, but I won't believe a word of it.* The well-prepared attack was launched – 'We had to come and disturb you, at this inopportune hour, to ask you something that might be entirely meaningless, but could just as easily provide the starting point for our investigations: investigations which, I need hardly say, will not affect you, your person ...' He went on: 'In one pocket of Sandoz's jacket, we found this card.' He pulled out of his own pocket a little rectangular, ivory-coloured card. 'On one side, typewritten, there is your name: CESARE AURISPA, PRESIDENT U.I. ... and on the other, in handwriting, *I'll kill you* ... a place-marker, as can be easily seen ... but the *I'll kill you*?

'A threat carried out there and then, you must have concluded. And, plainly, by myself in person.' The President laughed: an ironic, indulgent, bitter laugh.

The professional reserve of the Chief vanished immediately. He protested with vehemence: 'Whatever makes you say such a thing? For goodness sake ... I'd never forgive myself for thinking ...'

'Not at all,' said the President generously, 'you can forgive yourself. It's just that you've got it wrong: and we have seen too many men in your position fall in love with their mistakes, cultivate them like flowers, wear one or two in their lapel. It's normal, quite normal. That's how, some times, the most simple things in the world become damnably complicated ... your deductions were totally correct. That card marked my place at the dinner yesterday evening organised by the local cultural society named after Count de Borch; and it was me who wrote that *I'll kill you*. A little joke between me and Sandoz, as I'll explain. I gave the card to a waiter to take over to poor Sandoz, who was seated on the other side of the table, five or six places along from me ... The joke was that we were both pretending to be flirting with Signora De Matis, and since the lady, as had happened at other dinners of the same kind, had been seated beside him ... ?'

'You were pretending to be flirting, you say.' The Chief adopted a tone of disbelief, an incautious trick of the trade. The President, in fact, noticed it; and with a touch of disgust:

'You can take my word for it; in any case, just look at her ...'

'I wouldn't dare doubt it,' said the Chief. But the deputy thought to himself – you did doubt it, you are still doubting it: it's a credit to your profession, to our profession. In spite of his resolution not to speak, he directed a question at the President in the standard police form of a statement or assertion: 'And Signor Sandoz replied by writing on the place marker in front of him … ?'

The Chief looked over disapprovingly: as did the President, who seemed to become aware of his presence only at that instant. 'Yes, he scribbled a reply. He was playing the game … he said he accepted the risk, or something of that sort …'

'But you haven't kept the card.'

'I left it on the table. I might have stuck it back in the little ironwork stand; it was flower-shaped, if I remember correctly.'

'Whereas the unfortunate Signor Sandoz put the one you sent to him in his pocket: absent-mindedly, automatically,' said the Chief: scarcely concealing in the servility of the phrase a touch of incredulity, of suspicion.

'Exactly: absent-mindedly, automatically,' approved the President.

'What a problem,' said the Chief.

'Did you come here in the belief that I was the solution?' asked the President: ironic, annoyed, almost enraged.

'No, no, absolutely not. We came because it was necessary to clear up this detail, to get it out of the way at once; so as to be able to pursue other lines of enquiry.'

'Do you have any other lines of enquiry?'

'For the moment, none at all.'

'For what it is worth, and personally I believe it to be worth very little, I may be able to give you one.' He remained silent for some time, leaving the Chief in a state of anxiety which to the Deputy appeared too clearly expressed to be true: just as the president's face also turned too excessively expressive: with the promise of what he was about to reveal and, simultaneously, with regret for the puny content of the revelation itself. And indeed: 'It is not that it seems to me a line of enquiry with any real foundation; in fact it seems to me more of a joke: poor Sandoz too spoke of it as a joke …' (Another joke, thought the Deputy, these people spend their lives making jokes.) 'No later than yesterday evening, as we were making our way out of the restaurant, he told me he had received a threatening telephone call – perhaps one, perhaps more than one, I can't recall – from a … let me try to remember from whom, because it couldn't be … the words coming into my head right this moment are … *the Boys of Ninety-nine* … That can't be right: *the Boys of Ninety-nine* were the ones who were called up after Caporetto in 1917: "the Piave was murmuring", and all that …

Anyone of those boys still alive would be nearly ninety today: and in any case, it would be a reference to an indecently patriotic event ... No, no, it couldn't be ... Let me think ...' They let him think, until they saw his face light up with the relocated memory. 'That's it: *the Boys of Eighty-nine,* I think ... yes, eighty-nine ... But not the boys, now that I think of it: the children, perhaps ...'

'The Children of Eighty-nine,' the Chief savoured the words, but found there the bitterness of incomprehension. 'Eighty-nine, then. The children of the present year – 1989.'

The Deputy, who, observing the outcome of the President's efforts of memory, had thought that it would have been much easier to remember the year Eighty-nine, since only a very few days had passed since the New Year festivities, than the year Ninety-nine for all its associations with the Piave, found himself saying: '1789, more likely. A wonderful idea, that.'

Neither the President nor the Chief found this intrusion to their liking. 'You are always obsessed with history,' said the Chief. And the President said, 'What idea?'

'That notion of Eighty-nine. Where else does the idea of revolution spring from if not from that year? It does not take much now to admit that, as they used to say of a certain drink – it was the first and remains the best ... yes, quite wonderful.'

'Wonderful is hardly the word I would use.' The President gestured as though swatting a troublesome fly.

'Anyway, 1989 or 1789,' said the Chief, 'we will discover which in due course. Indeed I am confident we will know very soon ... What matters here and now, so as not to waste your time, which I know is valuable, is this; we must know exactly what poor Signor Sandoz confided to you yesterday evening about these Children of Eighty-nine and their threats.'

'For goodness sake, who said anything about confidences? He spoke to me with an offhand nonchalance. He was quite blasé about it. As I said, he was convinced it was a joke.'

'But it was nothing of the kind,' said the Chief: with a fondness for the Children of Eighty-nine which, for all its suddenness, gave every promise of developing bull-dog tenacity.

'I have nothing more to add,' said the President, rising to his feet. 'Try talking to other friends of poor Sandoz, or to his closest colleagues.'

'So,' said the Deputy, 'exit the President.'

'You'd prefer to hold him onstage?'

'Not exactly; it's just that I have a certain curiosity.'

'Keep it to yourself,' said the Chief: with irritation, brooking no opposition. As if to stress the point, he went on: 'I know them, these curiosities of yours: they are so fine as to be practically invisible to the naked eye.'

'Another reason for satisfying them.'

'Quite the reverse! I can't see them, and neither can any man of down to earth, common sense; but the people who are the object of these attentions, sooner or later they become aware of them. And then the troubles start, with a vengeance. For the curious.'

'I understand you,' said the Deputy. He was rambling somewhat. Since the pain had long since succeeded in taking a grip, giving him colours, images, and above all thoughts (but not in the night-time hours, during which it seemed to have no bounds but to penetrate every part of the mind and of the universe), he now felt and saw it as a slow wave in its ebb and flow; grey, leaden. But the conversation with the President, arousing him to a state of suspicious attention, had been a diversion which he was now prolonging in the conversation with the Chief. So as a blandishment to him: 'I am sure that you too must feel some measure of curiosity.'

'Let's make an exception for once: tell me about your curiosity, which you seem to think I share.'

'To know exactly what was written on the card Sandoz sent to Aurispa.'

'Yes, I just may be curious: but on a personal, whimsical level that has nothing at all to do with the investigation we are embarking on.'

'Are you curious or not?'

'I confess I am: but any investigation in this direction would hardly be viewed in a kindly light by the President.'

'He was so vague, so offhand concerning Sandoz' reply which, call it a joke if you like, was still the last thing written by a man who was murdered immediately afterwards ... I would say it was our duty to make enquiries: as a pure formality, nothing out of the ordinary. To tie up this business, in other words.'

'All right, I will drop you in front of the restaurant, and I'll send along two men to assist you in your search. But let's be clear about one thing: that card has no bearing on our enquiries.'

'You've got a line of enquiry already?'

'I will have: within an hour or two.'

'Dear God!' invoked the Deputy.

The Chief read the turmoil in his face: but restricted himself to a rancorous silence. Then, once they had arrived at La Nuova Cucina and the Deputy was on the point of getting out, he asked; 'What exactly fails to convince you?'

'The Children of Eighty-nine. If you let the word out, you know what is going to happen: all the way from Sicily to the Swiss border, they'll turn up in their dozens.'

'I won't say a word about them, if the friends and acquaintances of the victim do not oblige me with some confirmation, and with a few extra details thrown in.'

'I have no doubt that you'll receive your confirmation and extra details.'

'I have never seen you so optimistic.'

'On the contrary, I have never been so pessimistic.'

'I beg you,' were the words, but spoken in tones of authority, 'please do not make my poor head spin.'

The Deputy made a gesture of compliance and obedience. He went off to the café next door to phone the owner of the restaurant to get him to come and open up. While waiting, he had a drink.

The morning was glass clear and icy cold; as cold as the stinging pain in the joints of his bones. Nevertheless these eccentric, peripheral pains had the power to lessen the overwhelming central pain; or at least to give him that illusion.

He drank, one after the other, two cups of strong coffee. They said coffee deadened pain, but these coffees only gave him the lucidity to put up with it. His mind was, in the meantime, occupied with the refuse which would be in short time displayed before him. Garbage science. A parable, a metaphor: we are now concerned with garbage; searching for it, shaping it, reading it, seeking in it some trace of truth. In refuse. A journalist had once sought the secret of political secrets in the refuse of Henry Kissinger, and the American police the secrets of the Sicilian-American mafia in the refuse of Joseph Bonanno. 'Garbage never lies,' was now an accepted precept of sociology. But Bonanno's garbage had lied to police officer Ehmann: *Call Titone work and pay scannatore*. Nothing could be clearer, for Ehmann; if *scannare* in Italian means *to slaughter*, a scannatore is one whose job is to slaughter. It would have helped if he had known of *L'Aria del Continente*, the play by Nino Martoglio based on an idea from Pirandello, since it would have made him aware of the extent of the inferiority complex a Sicilian feels about his own dialect once he acquires a smattering of Italian. For this reason the Sicilian word Scanaturi had been, in the Bonanno household, Italianized to Scannatore. The jotting was no more than a note, an aide-memoire to remind the writer to pay a Sicilian-American joiner, Titone by name, for one of those huge, meticulously planed tables of strong wood on which the women – once in Sicily, now in America – knead the bread, make lasagne, tagliatelle, pizza or foccaccia. Scanaturi: 'an instrument for kneading dough', in the definition given, in the year 1754, by the Jesuit Michele del Bono. Had Bonanno naively Italianized the word, or had he set out to play a joke for his own benefit, on Ehmann?

Odd, thought the Deputy, that the word joke should have made its appearance with such frequency in these last hours. And it was a joke that he was playing on his Chief. He was certain that Sandoz' card would not be found among the refuse of the night before. And in fact, after two hours and more of searching, it was not found. *Garbage never lies:* in this case by absence. It was a different thought that unnerved him: that mankind was heading for death in a sea of garbage.

So as not to give the Chief headaches, he listened in silence to the interrogation of the friends and colleagues of poor Sandoz (whom, when alive, no one would have considered calling poor, rich as he was in talent, possessions, power and women; and there was every good reason for doubting whether he had in fact been assumed, a few hours earlier, into the heaven of the poor). Some confirmed the broad outlines, others added new details. Yes, poor Sandoz had spoken of phone calls from the Children of Eighty-nine; but as a joke, since, among other things, the last caller had seemed to him to have a child's voice – thin, hesitant, almost babbling. And he had spoken reflectively of the other calls, four or five in all, which, as he recalled, had seemed to him made by different voices, belonging to people of varying ages. All disguised, obviously; so perhaps it had always been the same person on the telephone, making the first call with an old man's voice and, regressing, the last with the voice of a child. 'The next time,' Sandoz had told his secretary, 'I'll get a call from a toddler.' He joked about it; he had even told the secretary that he had his suspicions about who was playing jokes of this kind on him. The Children of Eighty-nine: what an odd notion! And everyone, including Sandoz, had thought of 1989; new-born revolutionaries, which explained the falling age of the callers.

'As you can see,' said the Chief, 'your 1789 has gone for a burton.'

'Perhaps,' said the Deputy.

'Far be it from me to deny that your pig-headedness has shown itself, occasionally, of some value. But right now, trust me, it would be better to pack it away for better days.'

'I don't believe there will be a better time than this. But I have no wish to cause you headaches, or to upset you.'

'Go on, upset me.'

'All right. I believe that the joke – let's go on calling it a joke – was deliberately calculated to give rise to two successive hypotheses: the first, while Sandoz was still alive, and principally aimed at Sandoz himself, was that we were genuinely dealing with a joke – something innocuous and laughable; the second, once Sandoz had been murdered, that we were dealing with no such thing. For the first hypothesis, 1989, the comedy of people transforming themselves into the babes of some unspecified revolution, worked perfectly. What was it but a word, a mere word? For the second hypothesis, it is the threat, which begins to take concrete form with the murder of Sandoz, of imitating and rounding off the revolution of 1789, of renewing all its pomp and terrors, which works.'

'I am in agreement that the two jokes, as you prefer calling them, are linked.'

'Yes but there is another point on which we are not, and will not be, in agreement: that without our being aware of it, in the midst of the celebrations of the 1789 revolution, there was born a terrorist organisation utterly convinced of those principles, and now ready and dedicated to breaking the law to restore the part of that revolution which was once defeated; because this has to be the sense of the title Children of Eighty-nine. This association does not exist, but somebody wants to will it into existence, as a shield and a spectre for quite different purposes.'

'And who, in your view, had this wonderful idea? Wonderful was your word, right from the first; love at first sight, a *coup de foudre*,' said the Chief, with near hysterical irony.

'As to who had the idea, I do not know, and I do not believe we will ever know. But to judge from the effect it will in all probability produce, it is undoubtedly wonderful. Just think: now that the red flag no longer flies high, what revolutionary banner could be unfurled to seduce feeble minds, to attract the bored and the violent who need to dignify their instincts, or to appeal to those with a vocation for sacrifice and lost causes? I could add that your conviction that the children of Eighty-nine exist in the form they claim to proves just how brilliant the original idea was.'

The Chief turned serious, solemn and peremptorily decisive: 'Listen here; I let you have your way over the rubbish at the restaurant. A waste of time, both yours and of the two men, and God knows how much I could have done with them here ...' He sighed his habitual, long-suffering sigh over the shortage of men and equipment.

'I would not call it wasted time: the card, as I foretold, was not there.'

'All the worse; we wasted time in the full knowledge that it would be wasted ... Now listen to me: I am no fool; I can see your suspicions and intentions quite clearly, and I know what you are driving at and where you want to bring me. And I am telling you quite bluntly – No. And not only because I have no inclination for suicide, but because the line you are following is lifted straight from fiction, from one of those books they call a classical detective novel, where the sharp-witted reader can guess, after the first twenty pages, how it is all going to turn out ... Let's forget about the novels, shall we? We'll proceed calmly, with deliberation, without any brainstorms, without impulsiveness, and above all without prejudice or preconceived ideas ... In any case, the whole affair is about to be handed over to a magistrate: if he turns out to have the same taste in novels as you, you can put your heads together and speculate to your hearts' content, and I'll wash my hands of the entire business ... Meanwhile, I would like to point out that in the course of your lucubrations, you have overlooked one hypothesis which seems to me promising: that someone present at the banquet may have noticed that little game with the cards and may have seen Sandoz slip the *I'll kill you* into his jacket pocket; and that he may just have decided to take advantage of it.'

'A technically correct hypothesis, but, I believe, in the overall view of the matter, irrelevant.'

'You never know. Check up. Make the cultural association hand over the list of the guests, and find out who, among the diners seated next to Sandoz and the President, had the opportunity to watch the game. And next, obviously, who among them had any motive for detesting Sandoz. And finally, no brainstorms; not a step without informing me first. All right?'

Sandoz numbered an actor among his friends, and a colleague who remembered having seen them photographed together indicated him to the Chief as a possible perpetrator of the telephone joke. Since Sandoz had said he knew who was responsible for the joke, who could be more likely than someone with the professional ability? The actor had a certain reputation in the world of cinema and theatre, and the Chief recalled having heard him imitate a range of voices, from the guttural Catanian accents of Musco to the more polished, melodious tones of Ruggero Ruggeri. Without conviction, being now enamoured of the Children of Eighty-nine, he instituted a search the length and breadth of Italy for him. Finally they found him where they could have found him all the time, if they had taken the trouble to glance at the pages of the morning newspapers devoted to cinema and theatre.

Over the telephone, after listening to a cursory explanation of why he was being sought, the actor admitted that he had known Sandoz (a grudging admission, the only sort ever afforded to police questions), but not with sufficient intimacy to play jokes on him: and such a senseless joke into the bargain! Of itself, this served as the required corroboration for the police and the magistrature, who had taken over the conduct of the investigation, that there was a close connection between the phone calls from the Children of Eighty-nine and the murder. Meanwhile, as invariably occurred when responsibility for an investigation changed hands, the story about the Children of Eighty-nine leaked out. And obviously, since the year was 1989, almost all the newspapers assumed the name indicated a new-born, new style, different brand of terrorism. However, an anonymous phone call to the biggest circulation daily taxed the police, magistrates and journalists with ignorance and short sightedness, and pointed them in the direction of 1789. 'We will re-establish the Reign of Terror,' said the anonymous informant, adding that the execution of Sandoz – regrettably, not by guillotine – was only a foretaste of what lay ahead. A further call gave the group a more precise title: *Children of Eighty-nine, Saint-Just Action Group.*

'So you were right,' said the Chief. What he paid in wounded pride, he believed he was repaid in generosity: the generosity of a superior who gives way to his deputy.

'Yes, but this is not the point. The point is that the Children of Eighty-nine are being born now: of mythomania, of boredom, maybe of a vocation for conspiracy and criminal activity, but they did not exist a moment before the radio, television and the newspapers carried stories about them. The calculation of the people who murdered Sandoz, or who had him murdered, has created them. They calculated that at the very least they would confuse us, and that at best some fool would answer the call and proclaim himself one of the Children of Eighty-nine.'

'You've lost me. I cannot follow you in this work of fiction.'

'I understand. Anyway, even if you did agree with me, we would still be out on our own.'

A period of civic mourning and an official State funeral had been decreed for Sandoz, for who would now have had the audacity to lay to rest in a more humble tomb that victim of political criminality, of anti-democratic fanaticism and terrorist madness?

'I am glad to hear you acknowledge it: there would be no more than two of us, always assuming that your novel had the slightest element of credibility for me.'

'Just to continue with the novel ... we are facing a problem, a dilemma: were the Children of Eighty-nine created to murder Sandoz, or was Sandoz murdered to create the Children of Eighty-nine?'

'I'll leave it to you to solve that one. As far as I am concerned, and as far as this office is concerned, I proceed on the basis of established fact. Sandoz received menacing phone calls from the Children of Eighty-nine; Sandoz was murdered; the Children of Eighty-nine have claimed responsibility. Our job is to find them and bring them, as they say, to justice.'

'The Children of Eighty-nine.'

'The Children of Eighty-nine, precisely. And look; as regards that dilemma of yours, I could even, in an abstract way, as a game, as a purely literary concern, go along with the first of your two extremes: that the Children of Eighty-nine were born to dispatch Sandoz more conveniently and make our task in getting to the guilty party or parties more difficult, or even downright impossible. As to the second possibility, the one about Sandoz being murdered so as to give birth to the Children of Eighty-nine, I'll leave that one to you. And have fun with it.'

'For over half a century, in all branches of the police, we have had to swallow so many toads that I believe we have earned the right to a little fun. Apart from the many I have personally swallowed in nearly thirty years with this division.'

'One toad more, one toad the less ... What can I say? If you really see this business shaping up as yet another toad to swallow, get ready to swallow it.'

He was disobeying, being disobedient. In a little sitting-room in the De Matis house, with the lady herself at his side. She had sat down beside him, perhaps because curiosity had overcome her to the point that she instinctively imagined that physical proximity would create the best conditions for shared confidences.

'The moment the porter told me that a police officer wanted to speak to me, I understood: I have no doubt that you want to know about the cards that Sandoz and Aurispa exchanged three evenings ago.'

She had an intelligent face, and beautiful eyes which seemed to flicker with an amused, ironic light. Anything but unattractive. Aurispa had said that a glance at her was enough to make anyone aware that the desire to have her at your side could never be more than a game, a fiction, but that remark only revealed that he had the decidedly unsubtle view of female beauty of a purchaser whose only ambition was not to be short changed. She was thin but not displeasingly so; she could be said to be slight, and her movements and gestures were light and almost fluttery.

'I have to say at the outset that I am indeed a police officer, but I came to you in a private capacity and in total secrecy.'

'Tell me the truth, do you suspect him?'

'Do we suspect whom?'

'Him, Aurispa.' The amused, ironic light seemed to have spread out, adding a splendour to the eyes of indefinable blue, of indefinable violet.

'No, he is not a suspect.'

'It would give me enormous pleasure to know that at least the shadow of suspicion had fallen on him.'

'Really?'

'Yes, enormous satisfaction. And I still hope it will happen: there are so many murky matters in which he has a hand.'

'Why would it give you such satisfaction?'

'I could say to you: for the sake of justice, but it would not be the whole truth. Basically it is because I do not like him, I find him repulsive. He is such a cold man and he seems to exist only in profile, as though on a coin, on various coins.'

'Anything in particular?'

'No, nothing ... or rather, something, but something so vague that you cannot put your finger on it. But then, I always allow myself to be guided by vague, indefinite impressions, and I am never wrong, believe me ... but I see you won't be giving anything away. So let's see how good I am at making out what's behind your questions.'

Intelligent, very intelligent, thought the Deputy, and the reflection gave him a feeling of near panic. To gain time, to purify the questions of the suspicions which Signora De Matis was prepared to detect in them, he said: 'They are not really questions, the things I want to put to you.'

'Out with them, then,' said Signora De Matis, even more amused.

'I am engaged on an unremarkable, straightforward reconstruction of the last hours of Signor Sandoz. It is the sort of thing we are obliged to do even in those cases, like the present one, when we are convinced beforehand that it serves no useful purpose.'

'Unremarkable, straightforward ... serving no useful purpose.' The Signora's voice echoed his. She played her part in the game with ironic comprehension and indulgence, but also with barely restrained laughter. 'So what is the question?'

'As I said, it is hardly a question at all ... I take it you are aware that the two of them were engaged in a ... shall we say romantic game, at your expense. Aurispa regretted not having you at his side and pretended he was in the grips of uncontrollable jealousy because Sandoz twice in as many days had had the good fortune of a place beside you.'

'It had occurred more than twice. I could never understand why at those infernal official or society dinners they nearly always put me alongside that Sandoz – he used to bore me to death. Not only that, that little game of theirs, which you call romantic, bored me to distraction, or rather enraged me. It was as if they said to each other: Poor thing, she's so old, so unattractive that we really should give her at least this satisfaction. I do not need anyone to tell me that I am not pretty, and I am well aware that I am getting on in life, but that does not seem to me a sufficient reason why those two brainless creatures should dedicate a whole evening to letting me know it.'

'No, not at all, you mustn't think that,' said the Deputy, conscious of his own hypocrisy, because he had learned from Aurispa that things stood exactly as she had understood.

'Please, don't you start romantic games with me.'

'It is not a romantic game. You ... forgive me, it is the first time I have met you and I do not imagine we will have the opportunity to meet again; you are so radiant ...' The word came to him unbidden, as though he had fallen in love on the instant. The pain pressed in on him more and more sharply, as though to make him aware of the other, the only love now available to him.

'Radiant. Very gracious of you. I will remember that. There are not many joyful things left to one at this point in life. You know I am almost fifty ... but let's get back to the question, shall we?'

'Yes, the President sent the card over to Sandoz; written on it were the words ...'

'I'll kill you.'

'Did Sandoz write his reply on the same card?'

'No, he stuck Aurispa's card in his pocket, after giving it to me to read, with the delight, so it seemed to me, of a autograph hunter who has finally managed to secure a much desired specimen. He scribbled out his answer on his own place-marker, which was there in front of him, clasped onto a kind of iris which was too silvery to be genuine silver.'

'And what did he write on his card?'

'The odd thing was that he did not let me read it, and I had not sufficient curiosity to peer over his shoulder while he was writing. He simply bored me, as did that stupid game of theirs ...'

'Do you remember who Aurispa was sitting beside? I imagine he would have been seated between two women.'

'Yes, between two women: Signora Zorni and Signora Siragusa. But since Signora Zorni was seated on his right – you know who I mean; pretty enough, even if, to my mind, a bit empty-headed, but with just the right degree of empty-headedness to transform a pretty woman into a ravishingly beautiful one in the eyes of most men – he lavished more attention on her than on the other.'

'You saw the card arrive at its destination?'

'Not exactly: I watched Sandoz look over at Aurispa with great attention, with a sense of anxiety ... I had the impression he was studying the impact with much more interest than their futile little game warranted ... then I saw him smile. I turned to look at Aurispa, and he was smiling as well: but both wore a smile that was, how shall I put it? ... strained, sour ... That exchange of smiles between them made a deep impression on me: that's why, when Sandoz was murdered a few hours later, I asked if you in the police had suspicions regarding Aurispa.'

'No, we don't have any.'

'Then you should. Maybe it goes back to the first time I heard the word, and maybe it is just childish, but I still associate the police with the idea of polish ... you know what I mean ... cleanliness ... is there cleanliness in the police?'

'As far as there can be.'

'And as far as can be, there ought to be suspicions regarding Aurispa, but there is very little to be done, isn't that so?'

'Not a great deal.'

'If you tell me there is not a great deal to be done, I think it can be deduced that there is nothing to be done. The thing is that you appear to suffer over that.'

'I suffer over so many things now.'

'I would really love to know why you joined the police.'

'From time to time I ask myself the same question, but I have never managed to give myself a precise answer. Sometimes I unearth a dignified, high-minded reply, that soars upwards like a tenor's chest notes: more frequently the replies are more humdrum ... the necessities of life, chance, laziness ...'

'You are Sicilian, aren't you?'

'Yes, but from the cold side of Sicily: from a tiny village in the interior, among the mountains, where the snow lies for long periods in the winter. A Sicily which never figures in anyone's imagination. I have never again in all my life felt such intense cold as I did in that village.'

'I remember that cold Sicily as well. Usually we went in summer, but some times there were additional trips at Christmas. My mother was Sicilian, and her parents never left that village; they never ever moved from that great house of theirs which was cool in summer but bitterly cold in the winter months. They died there and my mother died there too, before them. I never went back. I receive a letter after every All Souls' day from one of my relatives telling me about his visit to the graves, about the flowers and candles he brings along to decorate them. It is almost a reproach to me, because, emotionally and sentimentally, the fact that my mother wanted to go back there to die ought to count for something. I am afraid the truth is that even this choice of my mother's, if I think about it, causes me some dismay. It is simply not possible to love a place or a people to that extent, especially when it was a place where you suffered so much, and a people with whom you do not have anything at all in common. My mother experienced only pain from her life there, and finally rebelled and fled, and yet she felt a love for it which went beyond the tomb ... And do you want to know why the thought of that gives me such a sense of dismay? Because every so often I bewilder myself by feeling an echo of the same love, of the same memory, of the same choice ... but perhaps it is only an expression of that remorse my relative is so anxious to make me feel.'

'I don't know if you have read that page of D. H. Lawrence's on Verga's novel *Mastro Don Gesualdo*. At one point he says: but Gesualdo is Sicilian, and it is here that the difficulty arises.'

'The difficulty ... Yes, perhaps that's where my difficulty in living comes from.' As if to change subject, very deliberately: 'You read a lot, don't you? I read very little, and now I find more enjoyment in re-reading: you discover things which were not there at the first reading ... I mean, were not there for me ... Do you know what I am re-reading? *Dead Souls*: packed full of things which were not there before; and who can tell how many other things I would find if I were to return to it twenty years from now? Enough of books. We were talking about the reasons which impelled you to join the police.'

'Perhaps, since crime belongs to us, to get to know it a little better.'

'Yes, it's true: crime does belong to us: but there are some people who belong to crime.'

Signora Zorni. Unquestionably beautiful, to the point of bland perfection; with a garulousness to match that perfection; head in the clouds, abstracted, afloat in the most celestial and unattainable heavens of a stupidity which she knows is both celestial and unfathomable; as do the genuinely intelligent, but they, experiencing that stupidity as a seductive force, fear it. She never seemed quite to grasp any question put to her, but the overall sense of the enquiry must, in some fashion, have nested in some recess of her beautiful head, since a reply could eventually be put together, even if it entailed picking and choosing the pieces which fitted best from a pile of multi-coloured stones, like a mosaicist. An operation the Deputy carried out as he went along, and we will follow suit; if it is to the detriment of the portrait, it is perhaps to the betterment of the narrative.

Yes, she knew about the half-pitying, half-mocking game which the two of them played on Signora De Matis: the President had informed her. She had seen the President write the *I'll kill you*, and had laughed at the idea, even if, she was anxious to add, she did not herself consider Signora De Matis as plain as many people thought: on the contrary, she was quite handsome, in her own way. And she had read Sandoz's answering card.

'Do you remember it?'

'Of course I do; I am blessed with a good memory as well.' That 'as well' spoke volumes for her confidence in her looks. 'It was two lines of verse.'

'Verse?'

'Yes, there were two short sentences written as lines of poetry; they even rhymed. They seemed to come from a song, and I had a terrible urge to hum them.' She began humming them for him, using the tune from a melancholic number in vogue several years earlier. 'I have no doubt that you will try: But who'll be victor, you or I?'

The Deputy felt a sense of exultation, but only said: 'The President read the card aloud, or gave it to you to read ...'

'No, he didn't give it to me; I read it while he was reading it himself. Then he slipped it into his pocket.'

'Are you quite certain about that — that the President put it in his pocket?'

'Absolutely so.' At that moment, a look of concern appeared on her face. 'Does he insist that he didn't?'

'Even if that were so, would you continue to be sure that he did?' His words were intended purely to cause her a moment of anxiety, to upset that icy perfection, reminiscent of a newly excavated, totally intact statue.

'He is a gentleman of such irreproachable ways that I would begin to entertain the tiniest doubt.'

'You can continue to be certain: the President claimed that he put the thing in his pocket mechanically; only he then, equally mechanically, threw it away.'

The Signora gave a sigh of relief, the carefully cultivated image reabsorbing that moment of life. The Deputy thought that she did not really deserve to be called stupid, considering that, according to current hazy opinion, it's not possible in Italy to brand anyone as stupid.

Leaving Signora Zorni's house, he felt numbed. Drawing precise replies from a speech that resembled the Trevi Fountain — cascades, sprays, streams and torrents of running water — induced in him a feeling of tension, followed by weariness and numbness. His pain too was numb, less sharp but more dull and diffuse. Strange how physical pain, even when its source is stable and, unless deteriorating, unalterable, can still grow, diminish, change in intensity and quality according to opportunities and encounters.

He walked under the colonnades in the piazza, his mind occupied with that card, with those lines from the song; with Signora Zorni, young and lovely, with a body of lithe harmony: but how much more beautiful and desirable — in those flashes of desire which momentarily pierced his pain — was Signora De Matis, for all her fifty years.

He relished the colonnades, and enjoyed strolling at ease among them. In the island which had given him birth, there was no city which boasted colonnades such as these. Arches make the heavens more lovely, in the words of the poet. Do colonnades make cities more civil?

It was not that he did not love the land where he was born, but all those invariably bitter and tragic events which day after day made the news there caused him a sort of resentment. Not having been back for years, he searched for it, behind mere occurrences, in his memory, in the emotion of something which no longer existed. An illusion, a mystification; as an emigrant, an exile.

7

There could be no half-measures with his disobedience. He had taken a chance with Signora Zorni, and the results would be apparent in due course. While neglecting to recommend silence to her – a recommendation which everyone, everywhere is irresistibly driven to break – he had none the less done everything in his power to convey the impression that his investigations were purely formal and superfluous, and a downright nuisance even for the people charged with carrying them out. It was, however, unthinkable that she had such a feeble memory as to totally forget, and, having not forgotten, that she would forgo the pleasure of informing one, two or more of her friends; and that from one woman to the next, the news would not reach the President's ears, and from the President the Chief's, or those of the occupant of a higher, much higher, position. Things stood differently with Signora De Matis: there was no such risk. Between the two of them, there had been the kindling of the spark of fondness, and a kind of complicity had been established.

From what he had heard about the exchange of cards, a question formulated itself in his mind, a question he had to put to a person able to provide a definite answer.

Kublai Travel Agency: proprietor, Dr Giovanni Rieti – doctor in what had never been satisfactorily established. An acquaintanceship of long standing, perhaps able to be considered a friendship, at least on account of the story of human tenderness which lay behind it. It had begun with their fathers in 1939: the Deputy's father, a local government officer in the Sicilian town where the father of Dr Rieti, a Jew, had happened to be born. Signor Rieti senior, in a state of despair, had come to the town from Rome, anxious to ascertain if in his birth certificate there might be some pretext for not considering him Jewish in the strict sense of the term. There being none, they – civil servants, mayor, Archpriest, municipal guards – made one up. Fascists to a man, each with party membership card in his pocket and badge in his lapel; if the Archpriest had neither card nor badge, he was Fascist in spirit. But all were unanimous that they could not abandon Signor Rieti, plus his wife and children, to the mercy of a law that was intent on his ruin. So they forged the documents in the duly accepted form, because to them the fact that a man was Jewish meant nothing if he were in danger, if he were in despair. (What a great country Italy was in these matters, and perhaps still is!)

They heard nothing more in his family of the Rieti family, and even if he retained some recollection of the case as one which had, among the many which had arisen in the first ten years of his life, made its mark, he had none the less forgotten the name. However one evening, in the city which had now been his home for some years, he attended a party in the prefect's office and there he was introduced to a Dr Rieti, who, on hearing his name, asked if he were Sicilian, if he were from such and such a town and if he had a relative who was in local government. It was like finding each other after years.

They met up on other occasions, with increasing frequency, until the Chief, with great tact and hinting at weighty matters left unsaid, advised him not to let himself be seen too often in the company of Dr Rieti. Still giving the impression of leaving the bulk of his information unspoken, he let it be understood that he had been tipped off by that service which in other times and in other countries would be called 'intelligence'; which perhaps here and now did not merit the title intelligent; but, be that as it may, who were aware of certain things and who in any case – this was the gist of the Chief's talk – 'knew each another', this being the very peak of the endeavours to which the Intelligence Services of every country dedicated themselves. Knowing each other, they knew Dr Rieti, and while it was permissible for them to be in communication with him, it was ill-advised for any other officer of the State, and especially so for a member of the police force.

The Deputy had continued to meet Dr Rieti, but with greater caution; he gave up meeting him for an aperitif in a bar, or for a meal in a restaurant, since suspicions regarding possible secret activities of his could arise if he spent his free time in the agency, if he were unusually well-informed on economic or financial deals, on internal rivalries inside the political parties, on the making and unmaking of alliances, on events in the bishop's palace or in terrorist circles.

On account of his illness, and of his work which took longer and became more of a burden as his illness grew more severe, he had not seen him for some two months. Dr Rieti greeted him with effusive cordiality, expressing his delight at seeing him in such excellent health. 'I knew you were not well. Some one from your office told me a couple of evenings ago. But you look all right now. A bit slimmer, certainly, but they tell us nowadays that losing weight does nothing but good.'

'You don't sound convinced.'

'I admit it. When I see what my friends and relatives have to do to lose weight, and the troubles they put themselves through, it's my view that all these various dietologists and inventors of diets should receive the same treatment as drug pushers ... what illness did you have, exactly?'

'To be exact, an illness for which I should be receiving cobalt therapy, or something of that sort.'

'I had no idea it was anything so serious.'

'It's even worse. I am dying,' he said, with such serenity that the other felt the words he was about to speak freeze from sheer insincerity. He muttered only a 'My God' quietly, then after a long silence: 'But a course of treatment ...'

'I have no desire to die fortified by the religious comforts of science, because not only are they as religious as the other sort but they are even more harrowing. If I were ever to feel the need of comfort, I would have recourse to the more ancient rites. In fact I would be quite glad to feel such a need, but I simply don't.' He continued in an offhand tone, almost with delight: 'Have you noticed? It is impossible to be bored in this country: we are all Children of Eighty-nine now.'

'Indeed, Children of Eighty-nine.' With irony, with malice.

'What do you make of it?'

'I think it is all so much hot air, pure fantasy. And you?'

'So do I.'

'I am glad you agree. I read in the papers that your office is taking the whole thing seriously.'

'Yes, of course. Do you expect them to miss out on such a splendid invention?'

'That's it exactly. It seems to me something invented round a coffee-table, as a game, as a calculation ... what is going to become of these poor devils, these poor idiots who want to continue believing in something after Krushchev, after Mao, after Fidel Castro and now with Gorbachev? They must be thrown some kind of sop, something which can be tossed back in the oven after two hundred years, something soft and scented with celebrations, rediscoveries and re-assessments: and inside the same hard stone to break the teeth.'

Always the same with Rieti: complete agreement over the evaluation of the facts, over their interpretation and the identification of their origin and purpose. Most frequently speaking of them hazily, by allusion, in parables or in metaphors. It was as if the same circuits, the same logical processes operated in both their minds. A computer of distrust, of suspicion, of pessimism. Jews, Sicilians: an atavistic affinity in their condition. Of energy. Of defence. Of suffering. A sixteenth-century Tuscan once wrote that the Sicilians are of a dry intelligence. So too are the Jews. But war had now descended on them: war by different means, but war none the less.

'I should like to ask you for the first time since we met – ' and with these words he revealed his knowledge of the real, secret activity of Dr Rieti – 'a precise question: what was the relationship between Sandoz and Aurispa?'

'They detested each other.'

'Why?'

'I don't know what set them off on their mutual detestation, and it is not something which it would be easy to establish, because from what I hear they were school-friends. I do know that they each dedicated themselves with a will – all the while maintaining a relationship of seeming friendship – Aurispa to ruining Sandoz's business and Sandoz, with less success, to ruining Aurispa's. The consequence was that Sandoz, who had no intention of settling for second place, decided on a policy of blackmail, but here too with negligible results. Obtaining a warrant for Aurispa's arrest, maybe even one which ended after a few months in an acquittal for lack of proof, had become the dream of his life. It never became anything other than a dream.'

'What were the grounds for blackmail?'

'I understand that the least ludicrous was based on a large scale act of corruption and fraud perpetrated by Aurispa against the State, for which Sandoz was in possession of proof, or believed he was. However I don't believe he would ever have gone to the length of making a statement to the police. There would have been reactions, counter-moves, and he would certainly not have emerged unscathed. Aurispa's only fear would be that Sandoz might have gone completely insane, because as long as he remained in possession of his faculties he would never have dared shake the columns, with the risk of bringing down the temple on his own head as well, their temple, the temple of so many Italians who matter ... The other grounds for blackmail were concerned with private matters, and they were at least thirty years out of date. Women, cocaine: what impression did he imagine they were going to make at this stage?'

'What about their business affairs?'

'War, war of every type. There is so much of it in the world ... and so much trade in arms, poisons.'

'Do I understand you to be saying that you do not see the hand of Aurispa in the murder of Sandoz ... let me phrase that better ... you do not believe that the threats issued by Sandoz would have constituted sufficient reason for wanting him eliminated?'

'Exactly.'

'Another reason, then.'

'You used the correct term: sufficient. Sandoz's threats did not constitute sufficient reason for Aurispa to want him out of the way, but at a certain point, when other needs became more urgent, in the preparation of some project or other which, when subjected to cool examination, did not necessarily require the elimination of Sandoz, well ... the opportunity presented itself, as the proverb has it, of killing two birds with one stone.'

'You mean that the victim could easily not have been Sandoz, but some one else with, what shall we say, equal qualifications? However, since Sandoz was more of a nuisance than any of the other candidates, the choice fell on him.'

'Exactly.'

'That is my opinion too. Immediately after listening to Aurispa, I said to my superior, who obviously takes no heed at all of my dilemma: the problem is whether the Children of Eighty-nine were created to kill Sandoz or whether Sandoz was killed to create the Children of Eighty-nine. And I tend to resolve my dilemma in the sense you indicate: that with one stone they have killed two birds: Primarily that of creating the Children of Eighty-nine ... but why?'

'As to why, I would say that through an ancient premonition, and a not so ancient admonition we know without knowing ... In our childhood we felt, rather than really knew, a power that today might be called total criminality, a power that, paradoxically, could be regarded as wholesome and healthy: always granted that it was crime, and comparing it to the schizophrenic criminality of today. The criminal nature of that power took the form principally of not per-mitting any other crime apart from the much vaunted, aesthetically embellished crime committed by itself ... there is no need for me to say that I prefer schizophrenia to good health, as I believe you do too. The important thing is that this schizophrenia has to be taken into account if certain otherwise inexplicable phenomena are to be explained. By the same token, it is vital to make allowances for the force of stupidity, of sheer stupidity insinuating itself and prevailing ... There is one power which can be seen, named and counted, but there is another which cannot be counted, which is without name or without names and which swims underwater. The visible power is in permanent conflict with the underwater power, especially at the moments when it has the gall to break surface with vigour, that is to say with violence and bloodshed: but the fact is that it needs to behave that way ... I trust you will not object to this piece of homespun philosophy, but where power is concerned, I have no other.'

'There are grounds for suspecting, in other words, that there is in existence a secret constitution whose first article runs: The security of power is based on the insecurity of the citizens.'

'Of all the citizens, in fact. Including those who, spreading insecurity, believe themselves to be safe ... this is the stupidity I was referring to.'

'Then we are tied up inside a *sotie* ... but let us get back to today's goings-on. Even if the newspapers have made no mention of it, you undoubtedly know all about the cards which Sandoz and Aurispa exchanged at that banquet as if it were a game ... what did you make of that?'

'It seemed to me a fact of some importance, but not one from which it would be possible at this moment to formulate reliable conclusions. A genuinely ambiguous fact, which could be clarified only by ascertaining the role of Aurispa in the whole business ... if he were the prime mover, if he were involved at the highest levels, he must have calculated that with that bit of nonsense over the cards he would, because of the way it occurred, have immediately been ruled out of the enquiries; if his part were secondary, it is also possible that he was not kept informed of the timing of the action; in that case it becomes feasible to believe in the chance nature of that game and in a fortuitous, and even fortunate, coincidence.'

'I would go along with the hypothesis that he was involved at the highest levels.'

'Perhaps, perhaps ...' said Rieti, but as though speaking out of courtesy. Plainly he knew something more, or believed he did. It was not right to press him on that point, so the Deputy said:

'One more question, perhaps the most indiscreet I can ask you: in your, let's say, functions, in the tasks you perform [the time for allusions was past; it was now the hour of truth for their acquaintanceship, or friendship, as for everything else] are you more interested in the business affairs pursued by Sandoz, until yesterday, or in those of Aurispa?'

'Of both, regrettably, although rather more, until yesterday, as you put it, in those of Sandoz;' with an expression in which the disgust for that business was possibly also disgust with himself.

8

He returned to find the whole police-station buzzing like a bee hive gone berserk. One of the children of Eighty-nine had been captured while making a phone-call. It turned out to be one of those cases which exist to defy all laws of probability. On the outskirts of the city, a deaf-mute was sitting on a park bench, three or four metres from a public phone-box inside which was a youth who, while talking, kept glancing nervously over his shoulder. For anyone other than a deaf-mute, accustomed to picking up the silent shaping of words on lips, the experience would have been like staring at a fish in an aquarium. He read a dozen times on the lips of the youth making the call the words – Children of Eighty-nine, Revolution, and Virtue. The deaf-mute happened to have in his hand a newspaper carrying reports of the Children of Eighty-nine, and in his pocket a marker pen with scarlet ink. He scrawled on the paper – Children of Eighty-nine – and went off in search of a policeman. He located a member of the local city force who was equipped with a pistol suspended from his waist, but who in every other way could hardly have been less suited to the job. He grew faint on merely reading the writing: he pretended not to take the business seriously, to regard it as a joke, to dispatch the deaf-mute with a little slap on the cheek. When the other, with the aid of dramatic and excited gestures, persevered, the policeman gave in and allowed himself to be escorted to the phone-box.

The youth was still inside and still talking: he was summarising for the benefit of the switchboard operator of some newspaper, duly trained in techniques of giving enough rope to callers of that kind, a chapter of Mathiez's *French Revolution*, which he had only just read himself. Since, to the best of his recollection, the police had never managed to catch anyone phoning to claim responsibility for terrorist crimes or for kidnappings, irrespective of the length of the call, he felt, although nervous, safe. The policeman waited behind a magnolia bush until the call was over, crept up silently behind the youth, then leaned heavily on his back so as to leave him in no doubt about the pistol pressed against his kidneys. Fortunately for both their sakes he had forgotten to remove the safety-catch. In this condition, closely followed by the deaf-mute, he marched him to the nearest police station; this turned out to be not particularly near, so he was obliged to declare on several occasions to the crowd which began to form as he made his way – and which had become a triumphal procession long before they reached their destination – that the prisoner was an alleged member of the Children of Eighty-nine: never forgetting, as the law requires, the word 'alleged', which is, as anyone familiar with current journalistic parlance will be aware, a synonym for established guilt. However, at a certain point, listening to the muttering of the crowd at his back, he found himself coming out in a cold sweat, fearing that their inclination was to implement swift justice rather than put up with the law's delays, with the risk that things might take an ugly turn for him, constrained as he would be to uphold the law's delays.

As God willed it, they arrived safely at a police station where all three – policeman, deaf-mute and child of Eighty-nine – were loaded into a van and dispatched to headquarters.

The youth was now in the Chief's office. Initially he had attempted to deny the content of the phone-call, but the deaf-mute was there at hand, implacably willing to write out the entire text, even if with occasional gaps. Finally, he caved in and made an admission, but insisted it had been a joke. That was not yet the whole truth, because he had believed that that call would have gained him admission to the Children of Eighty-nine, or at least advanced his candidacy. Joke or demented act of self-assertion, a glance at him was enough to make clear that he could not have been in any way implicated in the murder of Sandoz. This thought ran through the Deputy's mind the moment the door of the Chief's office opened slightly. The boy was in a state of collapse while the chief radiated, like a halo round his massive head, the weary satisfaction of the athlete who has breasted the tape first.

He closed the door gingerly behind him, barring the frenzied, avid stares of the reporters congregated in the corridor. Among them, preening himself and foaming like a thoroughbred stabled among pit-ponies, stood the Great Journalist. With his articles, from which the moralists without morals drank their fill week in, week out, he had acquired a reputation for being relentless and implacable; a reputation which boosted his price among those who felt the need to buy silence and freedom from obtrusive attention.

As the Deputy made his way towards his office, the Great Journalist stopped him and requested an interview: 'a brief one, very brief', he specified. The Deputy made a gesture more of resignation than of assent, while from the surrounding crowd murmurs of protest were raised.

'A private matter,' said the Great Journalist, to the accompaniment of a chorus of ironic, incredulous remarks – 'I bet', or 'Sure', or 'No doubt.'

In the office, seated facing each other – a desk covered with papers, books and cigarette-packets between them – eyeing each other in wordless distrust as though locked in a conflict to determine who could remain silent longest, the Great Journalist reached into his pocket for pencil and notebook.

The deputy raised the index finger of his right hand and waved it in a slow but definitive No.

'An automatic gesture, a professional reflex ... I have only one question to ask, and I do not expect an answer.'

'Then why bother?'

'Because neither you nor I are idiots.'

'I am very grateful ... What is your question?'

'This story of the Children of Eighty-nine, was it you in the police force who invented it, or was it handed to you prepackaged?'

'I will give you your answer: it was not us who invented it.'

'So they delivered it ready-made?'

'Could be ... that is my own suspicion, but it is no more than a suspicion.'

'Does the Chief believe that too?'

'I don't think so, but you'd do better asking him.'

The Great Journalist now wore a perplexed, mistrustful look. He said: 'I did not expect you to reply, and instead you did: I expected you to brush aside my suspicions, and instead you added your own. What's going on?' His mind, as could be seen from his face, was a morass of discarded ideas, of corrections, of rethinking and of hesitancy. 'So what is going on?' This time the words were tinged with anxiety.

'Nothing at all, I would say.' Then, to insult him: 'Have you ever heard of the love of the truth?'

'Vaguely.' He spoke with disdainful irony, as though cynically noting the insult were the only means of reacting to it: he was looking down on an individual far beneath his notice.

The Deputy returned to the attack with an 'Indeed, indeed', and added: 'Tomorrow, then, I expect to read an article of yours setting out all the suspicions and doubts which I, in my personal capacity, have just confirmed.'

The Great Journalist was red with rage: 'You know perfectly well that I will never write it.'

'Why should I know such a thing? I am still full of faith in humankind.'

'We are in the same boat,' His anger was tempered by a touch of frailty, of weariness.

'Don't you believe it. I have already landed on a desert island.'

9

The conversation had left him drained, but the pain had gone: it cowered like a beast – squat, ferocious and repulsive – lying in ambush in one sole point of his body, of his being. The final words of the conversation, however, left him with a yearning for the deserted island, for a spot where, as though huddled over some map, he could give free rein to an ancient dream and an ancient memory: in as much as certain things from childhood and adolescence were now ancient to him. *Treasure Island*: a book, someone had said, which was the closest resemblance to happiness attainable. He thought: tonight I will re-read it. His memory of it was clear, since he had already re-read it many times in that old, unlovely edition they had once given him. In the course of his transfers from one city to the next, from one house to another, he had lost many books, but not this one. Aurora Publishers: yellowing paper, which after all these years seemed to have left the print parched and faded, and on the cover, from the black-and-white version of the film, a scene featuring a feckless and lacklustre Jim Hawkins together with Wallace Beery's unforgettable Long John Silver. The same man had been equally unforgettable as Pancho Villa, so much so that after having seen both films it was impossible to read either Stevenson's novel or Guzman's work on the Mexican Revolution without the characters presenting themselves with the physique, the gestures and the voice of Wallace Beery. He thought of all that the cinema had meant to his generation, and wondered if it would have a comparable impact on the new generation, and whether that scaled-down cinema, totally insufferable to him, given on television could ever have any impact at all.

He returned to the island, and a new character, Ben Gunn, appeared before him. His mind was so free, so unfettered and capricious, that from Ben Gunn, via a detail he suddenly recalled, he moved on to think about the advertising industry that threatened to flood the world. Even the producers of Parmesan cheese undoubtedly paid their toll to advertisers, but not a single advertising executive had ever remembered Doctor Livesey's snuff-box. He gleefully imagined the poster or full-page ad that could be made from that scene: Doctor Livesey proffering, to potential buyers, the open snuff-box with a piece of Parmesan inside, just as he did in the narrative to Ben Gunn, himself a great lover of cheese. 'A delicious cheese, produced in Italy,' the doctor would be saying, or something of the sort.

Meantime, his eyes were fixed on *The Knight, Death and the Devil*. Perhaps Ben Gunn, from Stevenson's description of him, had some resemblance to Dürer's Death. The thought prompted him to view Dürer's Death as in a grotesque light. The weary appearance of Death had always unsettled him, as if it implied that Death arrived on the scene wearily and slowly at the point when people were already tired of life. Death was weary, his horse was weary, both a far cry from the horses of the *Triumph of Death*, or *Guernica*. Death, the hour-glass or the menacing pinchbeck of the serpents notwithstanding, expressed mendacity rather than triumph. 'Death is expiated by living.' A beggar from whom alms are begged. As for the Devil, he was as weary as the rest, too horribly demonic to be wholly credible. A wild alibi in the lives of men, so much so that there were moves afoot at that very moment to restore to him all his lost vigour: theological assault therapies, philosophical reanimation techniques, parapsychological and metaphyschic practices. But the Devil was tired enough to be content to leave it all to mankind, who could manage everything better than him. And the Knight: where was he bound for, armed from head to toe, so unshakeable of purpose, dragging behind him that weary figure of the Devil, and so hastily refusing Death charity? Would he ever struggle up to the walled citadel on high, the citadel of the supreme truth, of the supreme lie?

Christ? Savonarola? No, no, far from it. Perhaps what Dürer had placed inside that armour was the real death, the real devil: and it was life which, with that armour and those weapons, believed itself secure in itself.

Wrapped up in these thoughts, themselves affected by a strain of incandescent delirium, he had almost dozed off: the Chief, who came bursting into his office, found him in that state and said: 'You really are unwell.' Since he had become aware that the Deputy was failing and in pain, the Chief no longer sent for him when he had to talk to him: a kindness that the Deputy appreciated, but not without an element of annoyance.

'Not as much as I would like to be,' replied the Deputy, shaking himself awake, but feeling his pain reawaken too.

'What are you saying?' the Chief replied, pretending to be scandalised, but having understood perfectly well that the point the other wished to reach in feeling unwell was the point where he would feel no pain at all. However he was too blissfully happy to be side-tracked by anyone else's problems: 'Have you heard? What do you think?'

'Undoubtedly,' said the Deputy, with measured and gleeful malice, 'he deserves some punishment for what he has got up to: a charge, as well the obvious one of self-calumny, of giving misleading information, of conduct likely to provoke a breach of the peace ...'

'What do you mean?' This time not pronounced formally, but as a cry from the soul.

'I mean what I have meant from the very beginning: if we go along with this game of the Children of Eighty-nine, if we give a hand in creating them, this story will have no end; there'll be victims one after the other, and I do not just mean in the form of the corpses of murder victims, I mean people like the one you have in your clutches right now.'

'What do you mean?' once more, but this time heartfelt and almost imploring: 'What we have in our hands is a vital link in the chain, and you want us to toss it away as if it were worthless.'

'You're quite right: a link in a chain, but it is a chain of stupidity and human suffering, a chain of a quite different sort from what you have in mind. Be patient, listen to me for a moment ... This boy will carry on denying today, maybe even tomorrow, for a whole week, let's say for a month: but the day will come when he will confess to being a member of a subversive, revolutionary association called the Children of Eighty-nine. He will declare himself ready, no ... desperate to collaborate and, with our assistance, will provide the names of one, two, three accomplices, fellow members ... I wonder if he'll choose from those of his acquaintance he likes most or least; that's a psychological mechanism that would repay study, don't you think? ... In any case, we'll soon have further links in our chain ... By this time – you don't need much imagination to picture it – the police force will be out and about talking to professors, janitors, barmen, disco owners, managers of takeaway sandwich stalls – a new word, that ... it makes me tremble all over ... as though they had stuck together sandwiches and book stalls – Anyway, there they are busily interrogating, with the aim of getting as many names as possible of the people this young man saw regularly ... in the unlikely event of his obstinately refusing to talk, of his refusing to provide names, we would have no problem in picking one or two names at random from the list which will emerge from these enquiries ...'

'You really are unwell,' he said in a concerned, persuasive tone: 'Take a holiday: a couple of months off. You're due it; I'll see to it right away, if you like.'

'Thank you. I'll think it over.'

10

'Morphine is wonderful: it is essential to take it when you can't stand it any more,' a medical friend had advised him, handing over a little packet. The effects of a morphine dose were wonderful, more so when they succeeded an intolerable level of pain. The stronger the storm the greater the peace. 'Peace after the Storm', 'Saturday in the Village', 'The Solitary Sparrow', 'Infinity': Giacomo Leopardi, that poet happy in his unhappiness. What great and profound sentiments, expressed with utter simplicity and even with banal images had he revealed and stamped indelibly on the memory of that generation of Italians who could now be called ageing: in their far-off school years, and thereafter. Did they still read him nowadays in school? Maybe so, but there was certainly no child who knew his poems by heart. *Par coeur*, as the French teacher would put it, distributing the poems of Victor Hugo, almost invariably Victor Hugo. He could call them to mind even now:

> *Devant la blanche ferme ou parfois vers midi*
> *Un veillard vient s'asseoir sur le seuil attiedi ....*

> *Oh! combien de marins, combien de capitaines*
> *Qui sont partis joyeux pour des courses lontaines*
> *Dans ce morne horizon se sont evanouis...*

And he had them even more *par coeur* now. The sheer beauty of the expression, which he translated 'in the heart, from the heart and for the heart'. He discovered himself sentimental to the point of tears. But the doctor, with that sybilline, contradictory phrase, had only intended to warn him against dependency.

But what was the point at which a person just could not stand it any more? He pushed it further and further into the future, like some finishing-post in a contest between the will and pain. And not out of any fear of dependency, but from a sense of dignity in which the mere fact of his having been for the greater part of his life an upholder of the law, and of its proscriptions and prohibitions, played a part. He was well aware of what morphine was in a pharmacopoeia, in a hospital, in a doctor's bag or at the bedside of someone who had arrived at the point of being unable to take any more. Still, he could not quite bring himself to view it in the sunlight of permitted things, removed from the shadow of transgression and crime in which he, after years of practice, had been accustomed to considering it. The law. A law, he thought, however iniquitous, is still a form of reason: to obtain the objective of extreme, definitive iniquity the very people who willed and framed the law must themselves distort it and do it violence. Fascism was, among other things, this: a constant evasion of its own laws. So too was Stalin's communism – even more so.

And the death penalty? But the death penalty has nothing to do with the law: it is an act of self-consecration to crime, of the consecration of crime. A community will always, by a majority, proclaim the need for the death penalty, precisely because it is a consecration. The sacred, whatever it had to do with the sacred ... The dark pit of being, of existence.

Morphine, then. And a curious thought, prompted by curiosity, occurred to him: he wondered if in the year in which Tolstoy set the death of Ivan Ilich the use of morphine, for that purpose, was already known. 1885, 1886? It was reasonable to assume it was known, but was there any reference to it in the story? He thought not, and drew a kind of comfort from that reflection. Tolstoy was motivated by perhaps the same considerations as he was in refusing his character morphine. Thinking over that short story, he began to search inside himself for comparisons. Death as a quidditas, a quantum which coursed in the blood among bones, muscles and glands, until it found the niche, cradle or little cavity in which to explode. A minuscule explosion, a point of fire, an ember initially flickering, then of constant, penetrating pain: and it grew and it grew until, having reached the point where the body no longer seemed able to contain it, it overflowed into everything around. Only the mind, with its tiny, momentary victories, was its enemy, but there were moments, interminably long moments, when pain fell on every single thing, darkening and deforming everything. It fell on every pleasure which remained within reach – on love itself, on well-loved pages, on happy memories. Because it took possession of the past, too, as though it had always been present, as though there never had been a time when it was not there, when the body was healthy, young and given over to joy, in joy. Something resembling a satanic inversion of inflation was under way: those tiny reserves of joy which had been successfully put aside in the course of a life were being malevolently devoured by that pain. On the other hand, perhaps everything in the world took place under the sign of inflation; everyday the currency of life was losing its value: all life was a kind of empty, monetary euphoria bereft of purchasing power. The gold standard – of emotions, of thought – had been pillaged: the things of real value had now an unaffordable, if not wholly unknown, price.

Without having really decided, he was embarked on a search to check what was left of his personal reserves. He was walking along the banks of the river, stopping every so often to look at the muddy water, to watch life and time flow by.

He arrived at her house worn out: only one flight of stairs, of old stairs with low, smooth steps, but for him every ascent was now an exertion. Strangely, though, the exertion chased away the pain. He decided he must discuss it with a doctor; for all he knew there existed an exertion therapy; these days they discover so many, grow tried of them, rediscover them, only to grow tired of them all over again. The fact is that just as nature, with precious few elements at her disposal, is capable of forging an infinity of different faces, so it is, obscurely, with the intestines. What can a doctor know about all that? Even when there is the will to communicate to him that little which each of us feels – of the heart, of the lungs, of the stomach, of the bones – a doctor has no option but to refer it all to abstractions, to universals: even when everything is reported to him with the greatest of precision, like Proust in the dentist's waiting-room describing his toothache to Roditi, giving Roditi the consolation of discovering his own to be identical.

He rang the doorbell: carillon notes in the distance; something which always upset him, but more so now than ever. As usual, she came to the door a few minutes later, in the dressing-gown which, he was fully aware, she had slipped on that very minute. *Mais n'te promenes donc pas toute nue ... Never walk about completely naked*. He remembered, many years previously, in a small theatre in Rome (in Via Santo Stefano del Cacco, alongside both his office and that of Inspector Ingravallo, familiarly known as Don Ciccio Ingravallo; because such was the truth of the pages of Gadda's novel that he had the impression of having bumped into him on those offices rather than on the printed page), having seen Franca Rame walk about the stage, certainly not naked, and clad in a nightdress which was anything but transparent: because in those days transparent attire, let alone nudity, could provide one of his colleagues with the justification for girding himself in the tricolour sash and having the curtain brought down in any theatre. No longer: today clothes are removed without a second thought, in the theatre as in reality; and to think that in his childhood taking off one's clothes was considered the height of madness. 'He stripped himself bare naked': reason enough, if anyone appeared in that state, for the strait-jacket, the doctor's surgery, the asylum.

At home she walked about completely naked, to the delight, no doubt, as in Feydeau's farce, of the people in the building opposite, but causing him moments of scaring jealousy. Inside himself, now, he laughed at it, and so a sketch featuring the De Rege brothers (the theatre again) flashed into his mind. One of them came on limping with his head bandaged, his arm in plaster, blaming it all, it seemed, on 'jealousy'. The dialogue between the two went back and forth on the subject of the wife's jealousy until it became clear, in the course of the conversation, that those injuries were not the effect of an emotional spasm but of a fall from a *gelosia*, that is a shutter, a window shade ... the same word which also denoted jealousy. It may even be that the window attachment had been first dreamed up to ward off the tormented emotion of the same name, but the two had now nothing at all in common. It seemed that the emotion had been abolished in recent years, although possibly it was now making a come-back, but stripped of the overtones of tragedy: more redolent of ascetic preoccupations.

In the midst of these thoughts, which hardly deserved the name of thought, fleeting and pell-mell as they were, her amazement and momentary hesitation before recognising him caused him to see himself as though reflected in a mirror. The image, irrationally, irritated him profoundly, as though she had gone into her one of her, once adorable, little huffs. It lasted, like the regret for having returned to visit her at all, the merest moment.

'At long last,' she said. 'Where have you come from, what have you been doing all these months?'

'I was in Switzerland: didn't you get my letter?'

'A postcard,' she corrected him angrily.

'That's right, a card ... and this last couple of days in the office, I've been snowed under with work.'

'The Children of Eighty-nine?'

'The Children of Eighty-nine, among other things.'

'And this business in Switzerland?'

'A medical check-up. Very gruelling.'

'And what came out of it ...'

'All clear.'

He could see from her eyes that she did not believe in that medical all clear, but she had the shrewdness, the delicacy, the love perhaps, not to insist. She began to talk ramblingly about other things, but only about what had been happening to her during the period when they had not seen each other. She uttered no reproaches over his absence or his silence.

He stared at her, guessing at that familiar body underneath the flimsy clothing, that body he had loved and desired for years, never more than when she began to feel her youth passing and her body fading. Then she had felt herself menaced and offended, as though by an injustice or a criminal assault. At the same time there grew in him a feeling of tenderness which nourished and sharpened his desire. Desire and tenderness: all serene after the passion of the early years when their meetings were filled with problems and occasioned misunderstandings and resentments, from which pain and despair rose up like hurricanes. However, once the problems were ended, the passion was spent. Gone were those obsessions and agonies which she perhaps enjoyed but which he lived like one of those fevers where the rise and fall of temperature, of delirium and lucidity, mark the passage of days and hours. They always met with joy – the joy of their bodies, the only sort of which they could be mutually convinced; there was no need to ask more; they travelled together, at times undertaking journeys of unplanned variety and duration, although ever less frequently of late. Everything withdrew, everything was now far off. There remained in him that feeling of tenderness, now almost transformed into pity. Odd how in him now, every feeling which had been love or dislike was changed to pity. And even more odd how memory transfigured those far-off sufferings and depairs into beauty. Everything lied, memory included.

'What about these Children of Eighty-nine?'

'Somebody felt they were necessary.' Dürer's devil from the print came to mind. 'There has to be a devil before there can be holy water.'

11

'You seem more at peace,' said the Chief.

'Oh, as to peace ... as regards what is happening inside here, I would rather say that I have reached a state of indifference ... Forgive me if I speak to you in this way, with the sincerity of two equals: you are my direct superior and ...'

'Don't say that. I have always treated you as a friend, and I am aware of what is going on inside you, of your pain ... And as a friend, I want to put a clear, direct question to you: what do you want? From me, from us, from everybody involved in tackling this case.'

'Not a thing. At this point, nothing at all. I see quite clearly that things can only go in the direction they are going, and that it is impossible not just to turn back, but even to stop.'

'Tell me the truth: you wanted a warrant for Aurispa's arrest.' The fact that he now called him Aurispa and no longer the President was, none the less, a sign that he too felt, equally ardently, the same futile desire – to see a warrant issued for the arrest of Aurispa.

'Look: any time, in other places, thank God not in this one any longer ... any time I have had to execute warrants, I always felt like one of those sinister characters who – you remember the Stations of the Cross in country villages? – crept up to take Christ prisoner. No matter how vile the person to be arrested was, my state of mind was always the same ... Yes, it was necessary to execute the warrant: often, if by no means always, it was right; but I could never manage to get over that sensation.'

'It's a feeling which does you credit. But in our job ... forgive me for asking this, but why didn't you become a lawyer instead of a policeman?'

'Perhaps because I deluded myself that you could best be a lawyer by being a policeman ... Just take that as a joke. It's not true. People lie constantly, we do nothing but lie ... to ourselves more than to anybody else ... Anyway, no, I was not looking for a warrant for Aurispa's arrest, but I did want us to concentrate a little more on him, on his life and interests. And, more than anything else, I would have preferred us to pack that putative Child of Eighty-nine off home ... Where is he now, by the way? In isolation, I presume, in a cell two metres by three.'

'What do you expect?'

'Between friends, if you will allow me ... in all sincerity ... do you really believe that that boy has any part in some terrorist group which made its debut with the murder of Sandoz?'

'I wouldn't take an oath on it, but in the normal run of things ...'

'In the abnormal run of things,' the Deputy corrected him. To bring this useless discussion to an end, he went on: 'I took your advice. I handed in a request for a period of leave. For two months. I think that will be sufficient.'

'Sufficient for what?' asked the Chief, all ready with words of comfort and encouragement.

'To get my health back. What else?'

He went over to his office, opened the drawers of his desk and took out some letters, a packet of cigarettes and Gide's pocket edition of Montaigne, which he knew almost by heart. He left other cigarettes and other books. He stopped in front of the Dürer, uncertain whether to take it or leave it. He decided to leave it, indulging, with some relish, a fantasy over what would become of it. He imagined his successors regarding it as part of the furnishing of that office, like the map of the city and the portrait of the President of the Republic. Then someone would become aware of its status as Res Nullius, would carry it triumphantly home or, possibly, to an bric-à-brac stall, where a dealer would discover it and the whole itinerary by which things end up at nearly chic auction sales would be underway all over again. At least in this way it would come to the attention of lovers of such things, or to one lover, someone like him, perhaps; an extemporised, in-competent lover.

He strolled around the city, relishing a sense of freedom which he never remembered experiencing before. Life retained all its beauty, but only for those who were still worthy of it. He felt himself to be not unworthy, indeed to be almost among the selected. It was time to cry out: 'God hath given you one face, and you make yourselves another': not in the spirit of Hamlet to women, with their cosmetics, face-creams or lipsticks, but to all who merited the tag 'unworthy', to the whole worthless mass who were multiplying day by day and filling the earth. He burned with the wish to bellow to the world that this was its new essence – that it had shown itself unworthy of life. But had not the world, the human world, always obscurely aspired to being unworthy of life? An ingenious and ferocious enemy of life, of itself, while at the same time the inventor of so many benevolent forces – law, rules of play, proportions, symmetries, fictions, good manners ... 'The ingenious enemy of myself', the dramatist Vittorio Alfieri had said of himself, of himself the man; but equally the ingenious friend, at least until yesterday. As usual, however, when he arrived at the misery of today and the despair of tomorrow, he wondered whether in deploring the indignity into which the world was sinking there was not an element of rancour at being about to die, and of envy towards those who would remain. Perhaps it was so, even in the midst of the all-embracing pity he felt for those who would remain: so much so that at certain moments, embittered, he found himself repeating to himself, like the compères of Variety shows in his younger days, a 'Have a wonderful time, ladies and gentlemen': like a farewell greeting, scoffingly. None the less, in the awareness that there would be no 'Wonderful time', there was, however perversely, a hint of pity.

He was now walking through the park. The children, yes, the children: so graceful, so much better fed than previously (the frail and hungry childhood of those who were now elderly), perhaps more intelligent and undoubtedly, overall, better informed: yet he had for them an enormous compassion and apprehension. Will they still be here in 1999, in 2009 or in 2019, and what would this succession of decades bring them? Immersed in these thoughts, he realised he had reached, as it were, the threshold of prayer, which he glimpsed as a deserted, desolate garden.

He stopped to follow their games, to eavesdrop on what they were saying to each other. They were still capable of joy, of imagination, but lying in wait for them was a school without joy and without imagination, the television, the computer, the car from home to school and from school to home, and food which was rich but as tasteless as blotting paper. Never again, committed to memory, the multiplication tables, the poems ... 'The maiden from the country came...' or else 'All trembling on the threshold ...' or even 'The cypresses which at Bolgheri ...' – torments of other times. Memory was to be abolished, all Memory; and similarly those exercises which aimed at making it flexible, subtle or retentive.

In the small towns, children could still enjoy the same freedom as before, but in the cities everything, by necessity and science, was like a battery-hen farm. Some were intent on having them born as monsters, perhaps prodigious monsters, for a monstrous world. 'What we are doing,' a famous physicist had once told him, 'is all flowers and roses compared to the things biologists are up to.' He was somewhat confused by the expression 'flowers and roses', as though the rose, by virtue of literature, had been separated from the genre 'flower'. The roses I failed to pluck, he thought to himself. But it was not true, it is not true that life is made up of missed opportunities. No regrets.

A dog, an Alsatian with a good-natured, worn-out appearance, had approached a pram in which a fair-haired baby was peacefully asleep. The girl who was supposedly looking after the child was engaged in a conversation with a soldier. On an impulse he went over and positioned himself between the dog and the pram. The girl left off talking to the soldier, threw him a reassuring smile and, gazing affectionately in the direction of the dog, said it was an old, friendly thing which would never harm a living soul. He continued on his way and, noticing how many dogs were roaming around the park, attempted to count them. So many dogs, perhaps even more than the multitudes of children. What if the slaves were to count themselves, Seneca had once asked. Supposing the dogs were to count themselves? There had one day appeared among his routine cases the horror of a child savaged by a Great Dane. The family pet: no doubt old, friendly and never harming a living soul, just like the girl's Alsatian. Looking round at the many children running through the park, and at the countless dogs which seemed to be running alongside them or watching over them as they played, that case from long ago came back to mind and brought an apocalyptic vision. He could feel it on his face like an unclean, clinging spider's web of images. He lifted his hand to wipe it off, warning himself to die better. The dogs were still there, too many of them; they had nothing in common with those which, his father being an avid hunter, had been around him in his childhood. Small dogs, those, a pack of squat, Sicilian mongrels; always playful, tails wagging, filled with a love of the countryside rather than of the hunt. These dogs, on the other hand, were enormous, doleful creatures, their minds seemingly set on thick, dark woods or impenetrable stone quarries. Or Nazi concentration camps. In any case, for anyone who gave it any thought, it was clear there were too many of them everywhere. And too many cats. And mice What if they were to count themselves?

That obsession fading, he passed from one thought to the next and began to recall the dogs of his childhood, their names, the prowess of some, the laziness of others – in the very way that his father had talked about them in conversation with fellow hunters. A thought which had never previously occurred to him now suddenly flashed into his mind: not one of them had died at home. None of them had been seen dying or found dead in their basket of straw and old blankets. At a certain stage in life, or at a certain stage in the progress of their bronchitis, it had been noted that they had no further taste for food or play, and they simply disappeared. The shame of themselves dead. As in Montaigne. And the fact, asserted almost as the Kantian imperative, as an illustration of that imperative, that one of mankind's highest intelligences, in his wish that death should come to him, preferably in solitude but at least far away from those who had been close to him in life, had by meditation and reasoning attained what the dogs instinctively felt, seemed to him sublime. This train of thought, mediated by the great shadow of Montaigne, succeeded in reconciling him with the dogs.

12

After one of his more peaceful nights, with pain awakening him at the end of dreams in which something or someone seemed to be continually beating him on the side, on the shoulder or on the neck, he passed the following morning with his newspapers, magazines and books. The Great Journalist had written an article in which he bitterly accused the police and security services of having fostered the re-emergence of the cancer of terrorism, and of having realised what had happened only when they were confronted with the corpse of poor Sandoz in the morgue. The Catholic journal, *The Pilgrim*, published a lengthy article dealing with the wickedness of the '89 and of these its blessèd offspring of today. They were not exactly called blessèd in the article, but since they were engaged in killing, a certain measure of understanding and indulgence, in anticipation of final forgiveness, had to be afforded them.

The pain appeared to be dimmed and to have taken on the semblance of a milky, off-white substance. He finished re-reading *Treasure Island*, which still resembled happiness. He was on the point of replacing it on his bookshelf when the woman who came every morning to tidy up what little that there was to tidy up arrived. She had not expected to find him at home, and asked if he were not well or if he had decided to take a break.

'A break, a short break.'

'Good for you,' she said: there had been, in the course of the morning, a murder, something really big. It was not hard to imagine how busy the police would be.

He asked about the murder as he rushed over to switch on the radio. The woman said that the victim was a friend of the man who had been killed a week ago, but she could not remember his name.

There was not, in all the hubbub of music and chatter which the radio dispensed, a single voice giving any news. He switched it off.

To make up for the silence of the radio on the murder, the woman did her best to remember.

'It was the name of a town in Southern Italy.'

'Rieti?'

'Yes, that's it, Rieti.' The woman brightened up at the recollection. She thought to herself: these people know everything that is going to happen before it does. She too, although proud of her Northern origins and not from Southern Italy, was harsh in her judgements on the police.

A friend of the man who had been killed a week previously, the name of a town in Southern Italy: the name Rieti had immediately occurred to him. Now more than pain, stronger than pain, a feeling of defeat overcame him. He felt as though entangled in one of those detective stores where the author, without warning, uses and abuses the reader, with crass duplicity which never even manages to be clever. Except that, in this case, the duplicity was a mistake, a mistake of his. Had it possibly also been a mistake of Rieti's? Or had Rieti hidden that part of the factual truth in which he was most directly interested?

He spent hours turning it over in his mind, as though engaged in an endless game of patience in which something always went awry: one card which refused to be fitted into place, one space into which the awkward card could not be placed.

He left his house as night, mixed with fog, was falling. He headed, without having decided on it – like a donkey for the stables, he thought when he noticed what he was doing – for the office.

He heard the shots, or so it seemed to him, an incommensurable time before feeling himself hit. He fell thinking: you fall as a precaution and as a convention. He believed he could rise to his feet, but found himself unable to. He raised himself on an elbow. Life was draining out of him, effortlessly, in a flow: the pain was no more. The hell with morphine, he thought. Everything was clear, now: Rieti had been murdered because he had spoken to him. At what point had they started following him?

His elbow had no longer the strength to support him and he fell back. He saw the lovely, immobile face of Signora Zorni light up with malice. He watched it fade away, at the end of the time whose threshold he was even now crossing, into the headlines of the following day's papers:

CHILDREN OF EIGHTY–NINE STRIKE AGAIN.

COLD–BLOODED MURDER OF INVESTIGATING OFFICER.

He thought: what confusion! But it was now, eternally and ineffably, the thought of the mind into which his own had dissolved.

ONE WAY OR ANOTHER

Translated by Sacha Rabinovitch

Since in truth the primal cause of all things can be expressed in many words, in few and even in none insofar as it cannot be said or understood, seeing that it transcends everything super-substantially and shows itself truly and unveiled only to those who are beyond that which is impure as well as that which is pure, and who rise above all the holiest peaks and forsake all the divine lights and the sound of heavenly words, and plunge into the darkness where, as Holy Scripture says, He who is above all things truly stands . . ., we can say that this cause is neither soul nor intellect; that it has neither imagination nor opinion nor reason nor thought, and is not reason or thought, and cannot be expressed or thought. It is not number or order or greatness, smallness, equality, inequality, similarity, dissimilarity. It is not in motion nor motionless, nor at rest, nor has it power, neither is it power or light. It does not live nor is it life: it is not substance nor age nor time; of it there is no intellectual perception. It is not knowledge and it is not truth, nor royal authority nor wisdom; it is not one nor divinity nor good, it is not spirit according to our concept of spirit. It is not filiation nor paternity nor any other thing known to us or to any other being . . . It is none of those things that pertain to non-being nor of those that pertain to being, nor do beings know it such as it is in itself, just as it does not know beings insofar as they are beings. No idea of it can be given nor name nor knowledge; it is not darkness and it is not light, it is not error and it is not truth.

—Dionysus the Areopagite, *De mystica teologia*

I let fall the last veil of modesty, quoting Saint Clement of Alexandria.

—Casanova *The Story of my Life*

The greatest Italian critic of our time has written: 'If, as a famous definition puts it, the Kantian universe is a chain of causalities suspended on an act of freedom, we could likewise say that the Pirandellian universe is endless slavery in a world devoid of music suspended on an infinite musical potentiality — on the unimpaired fulfilled music of *an isolated man*'.

I believed I'd retraced a whole chain of causalities. Reached, as isolated man, the infinite musical potentiality of those childhood or adolescent experiences when, in the summer in the country, I used to retire for long hours to some spot which became in my fantasy remote, inaccessible, full of forests and streams and my whole life, its brief past and long, long future, merged musically and endlessly with my present freedom. And for a number of reasons — not least that I was born and had lived for years in Pirandellian landscapes, among Pirandellian characters, with Pirandellian traumas, so that between the author's text and the life I'd led till I grew up there wasn't a gap either in my memories or my feelings — for a number of reasons, that critic's words rang in my head (with such persistent clarity that I can now transcribe them from memory without checking) rather like a phrase or a theme of that infinite musical potentiality I'd achieved. Or thought I'd achieved.

In other words I had no occupational or sentimental obligations. I was just about able to satisfy more or less (I liked to think it was less) every need or whim. I had no commitments or goal (apart from the casual requirements of eating and sleeping). And I was on my own. No anxieties, no apprehensions. Except for those, obscure, irrepressible which always pursue me, about life and living. On to which were grafted

59

and from which stemmed an anxiety, an apprehension related to that act of freedom I couldn't avoid — but slight and slightly numb. It was as though I'd been caught in a play of mirrors, unobtrusive yet luminous and calm like the time of day and the landscapes through which I drove, set up to reflect and multiply — when it happened, when I would choose to make it happen — my act of freedom.

I was travelling by car. And this means of locomotion which I hate and rarely employ had, from the moment I decided to be free, come to be part of my freedom. I drove at a leisurely pace with a composure that rendered harmless my more or less constant lack of concentration. And this moderate speed together with the tranquil pleasure of looking about me as I drove were what enabled me to glimpse on a bend the sign: Zafer Hermitage, 3 — black on yellow. Which my anxiety, my apprehension immediately seized on like a bait. I stopped the car and let it glide slowly back till I was alongside the black and yellow sign. Zafer Hermitage, 3. The word hermitage, the name Zafer, the number 3 were all equally and diversely significant for me — not to mention the significant fact that they were three, a further three, and that I'd been roaming freely for just three days. (Need I confess that I'm subject to a slight but tenacious trinity neurosis, whose origins and persistence I can't explain?) A hermitage is a place for solitude — not for that objective, country solitude we usually discover and appreciate when we are in company: a lovely, lonely spot, as we say, but for a solitude that has mirrored a different, human solitude and is tempered with emotion, meditation, perhaps madness. As to Zafer: some Muslim or Christian hermit? And moreover it was three kilometres away, no more and no less. I performed the simple manoeuvre required to penetrate the narrow tarmac lane (the tarmac ought to have put me on my guard) and began to climb the slope. Cork-oaks and chestnut trees formed an arcade, the air was filled with the scent of late broom. Then all at once a vast esplanade, also covered in tarmac, one side of which was shut off by a huge concrete barracks hideously pierced with narrow oblong windows. I drew up, disappointed, furious. Since there was no sign of the road continuing, this horrible building must be the hermitage. A hotel most likely. And I remained undecided for a while whether to turn back without getting out of the car or to get out and try to discover who had planted that great barracks of a building there and why. Curiosity prevailed. Besides the desire to compensate for my disappointment a little by letting somebody know — there had to be somebody there even if the place looked deserted and if there wasn't a sound to be heard – how indignant I was at finding instead of a hermitage a hotel. I got out and locked the car, for there was something ominous about that silence. The front door of the building, wide and glazed, was open. I went in and, as I'd expected, found myself in the entrance hall of a hotel. At the porter's desk, behind which was the usual nest of pigeon-holes hung with keys, sat a priest — young, dark, long-haired. He was reading *Peanuts*. Seeing me his face fell with annoyance. He replied to my greeting soundlessly, moving his lips.

'Excuse me, is this a hermitage or a hotel?' I asked with almost aggressive irony.

'It's a hermitage and a hotel.'

'The Zafer Hermitage?'

'The Zafer Hermitage, precisely.'

'And the hotel?'

'The hotel what?' Very annoyed.

'What's the name of the hotel?'

'Zafer,' and stressing each word to imprint it on my memory: 'Zafer Hotel.'

'Zafer Hermitage, Zafer Hotel. Good. And who was Zafer?'

'A hermit obviously. Since this was a hermitage.'

'Was,' I observed.

'Is.'

'It's you who said was . . . However. A Muslim hermit?'

'Muslim indeed! Do you suppose we'd have gone on com-memorating a Muslim?'

'Why not? Ecumenicalism . . .'

'Ecumenicalism has nothing to do with it . . . He was a Muslim, then he converted to the true faith.'

'The true faith. But that's a Muslim expression.' I wanted to

61

go on teasing him.

'Perhaps,' said the priest. And he resumed his reading of *Peanuts* to make it quite clear that I annoyed and disturbed him.

'If it's not too much trouble,' — making it as obvious as possible that that was precisely what I hoped it was — 'I'd like to know something about Zafer, about the Hermitage . . . and about the Hotel.'

'Are you a reporter?'

'No. Why?'

'If you're a reporter you're wasting your time. The scandal's over and done with.'

'Scandal?'

'About the Hotel. That it oughtn't to have been built. That it's ugly . . . It's all over. Three years ago.'

'I'm not a reporter. And I'd also like to know something about the scandal.'

'Why?'

'I've nothing to do. Nor have you it seems.'

He cast a now resigned glance at *Peanuts*. 'As a matter of fact,' he said, 'there are things I should be doing.'

'What?' I asked impertinently, aggravatingly.

'Oh . . .' he said with a vague gesture towards the many things he had to do, the endless confusion into which he'd have to plunge for who knows how long and at what cost — so that in the mean time, to keep himself fit for the test he read *Peanuts*.

I told him as much. He was visibly nettled but his tone became friendlier.

'What can I say? About the scandal, about how matters were described by some newspapers, some politicians, I know very little . . . It happened, and that's it . . . There was this hermitage, a ruin, a little abandoned church. Then three years ago Don Gaetano built this hotel . . . The Republic watches over the environment, of course, but since Don Gaetano watches over the Republic . . . In fact the usual thing.' He smiled bitterly. It was hard to tell whether it was Don Gaetano or the Republic he resented.

'And who is Don Gaetano?'

'You don't know who Don Gaetano is?' Amazed, incredulous.

'I don't. Should I?'

'I think you should.' He was beginning to enjoy himself.

'Why?'

'Because of what he's done, what he does . . .'

'He made this hotel. Are all the things he does of this sort?'

'He made this hotel with his left hand so to speak.'

'And with his right?'

'Schools. Scores of them, hundreds perhaps. All over the place. Every type of school. Even a university.'

'Hundreds of schools and a hotel.'

'Three hotels.'

'Well, three hotels. And always by pulling down a hermitage?'

'He doesn't pull down hermitages. He incorporates them. Here the Zafer Hermitage is intact. It's become the crypt.'

'Can it be visited?'

'Of course it can.' He sighed wearily, expecting me to ask him to show me round it.

I didn't ask. 'And Don Gaetano?' I enquired.

'Don Gaetano what?'

'Can one visit Don Gaetano?'

'Of course. He's here. For the whole summer. Of the hotels he's built, this is his favourite.'

'Why?'

'I don't know. Childhood memories perhaps. Perhaps because the building of it required the longest battle. But he won it.'

'Obviously. He couldn't fail to win.'

'Yes indeed. He couldn't fail to win,' he agreed. He sounded proud and just a little reticent.

I looked around. 'It certainly is peaceful,' I said. 'Is it comfortable?'

'The Hotel? Extremely comfortable.'

'I might stay a few days,' I said.

'That's not possible.'

'Full up?' Ironically, since it seemed, and was, deserted.

'For the moment we're twenty-one, including staff. But the day after tomorrow it'll be full.'

63

'Your guests all arrive together?'

'They're special guests.' He paused. Then as though confiding a secret: 'Spiritual exercises.'

'Ah ha. Spiritual exercises!' With an air of astonishment that befitted the confidence. But I really was rather astonished. For years, a great many years, I hadn't heard mention of spiritual exercises. I thought they were no longer practised. When I was a boy everybody talked about spiritual exercises whenever the Mission of St Paul came to our town. It was an important annual event, comparable to the arrival of the operetta troupe of Petito-D'Aprile and the theatrical troupe of D'Origlia-Palmi. And just as regular. The Mission's sermons were for everybody, but their spiritual exercises were for the chosen few. Finally they would plant an iron cross in memory of the Mission somewhere on the outskirts of the town and go away. The last time I heard of spiritual exercises was just after the war. The elections were drawing near, the first, and a Dominican father had come to preach. He had inspired such enthusiasm in the clerical and educational community that they had gathered around him for a whole week in a villa some wealthy devotee had put at their disposal. And the funniest part of it was that even the freemasons went, and in the end they were won over body and soul, like those who were not masons.

'Spiritual exercises,' the priest repeated. 'Every year, regularly. The sessions begin on the last Sunday in July.'

'And how long does a session last?'

'A week.'

'And how many sessions?'

'Three, four. Three up to last year, four this year.'

'The faithful are on the increase.'

'Undoubtedly,' the priest agreed — for the sake of appearances. He wasn't so sure. Then, confidential again: 'But the first session is the most important.'

'Why?'

'On account of those who take part.' And, lowering his voice to make it yet more confidential: 'Ministers, Deputies, Chairmen and Bank Managers, Industrialists . . . And three Newspaper Editors as well.'

64

'Bigshots,' I said. 'I'd give a lot to be here when they do their spiritual exercises.'

'That's impossible.'

'I understand . . . But today and tomorrow, until the hotel, as you say, is full, I might stay mightn't I?'

'In principle . . .'

'And in practice?'

'In practice, always allowing that Don Gaetano consents, you'd have to make do, to manage as best you could. The service leaves much to be desired. As to the cooking . . .'

'Would I be the only paying guest, so to speak?'

'Not the only one. There are five others.' Then simultaneously exasperated and mysterious: 'Five women.'

'Old and foreign,' I said.

'Not at all. They're neither old nor foreign.'

'But alone?'

'They arrived alone.' As though declining all responsibility. But with a roguish glint in his eye.

'But you're not sure they really are alone.'

'No, no.' Feebly in an attempt to make amends. 'I mean they arrived alone but now they keep each other company.'

'So I'd be the sixth.'

'We must see what Don Gaetano has to say.'

'Let's see.'

'Not now. Later, when it's time for lunch. He mustn't be disturbed when he's meditating. He's in the chapel downstairs.' He gestured towards the floor.

'In Zafer's Hermitage,' I said.

'Precisely. In the meantime you can circulate freely — indoors, outside.' Our conversation was definitely concluded. His eyes hungrily sought *Peanuts*.

I went outside. Beyond the esplanade, into the wood. The trees grew denser, the air fresher and resin-scented the further I got from the hotel. Here was perfect solitude. I was thinking of all the perfection and of the freedom in which I enjoyed it when, through the foliage, I glimpsed a lake of sunshine dotted with bright colours. I drew nearer cautiously. In the sunny clearing were some bikini-clad women. Five to be precise.

65

Without a doubt these were the women whom the young priest had mentioned. I came closer still, noiselessly. And they too were silent. Four stretched out on their brightly coloured bathtowels, one sitting up, absorbed in a book. It was a vision. Something mythical and magic. If one pictured them completely naked (which required no effort of the imagination), the result was a painting by Delvaux (not by me — I've never been able to see women as mythical or magic, nor thoughtful, nor dreamy). The manner in which they were disposed, the perspective from which I perceived them was pure Delvaux. As well as what couldn't be represented but which I knew: the fact that they were alone in that gloomy barracks of a hotel run by priests. I stood there for a while spying on them. They had fine figures. Four were blonde, one dark. I couldn't tell if they were pretty because of the enormous sunglasses they wore — and because of the distance, too, despite my longsightedness.

I must admit that I fancied an affair. And that I was as happy picturing myself in their midst as I'd been earlier savouring the perfect solitude — if not happier. But I retreated and went back to the hotel.

I found Don Gaetano (it could only be him) leaning against the outer edge of the desk behind which the porter-priest was reading, instead of *Peanuts*, a black-bound book. Tall in his long cassock, motionless, his gaze distant, steadfastly vague, a rosary of big black beads clasped in his left hand, the right, large and almost transparent, on his breast. He appeared not to have seen me, but came to meet me. And still seeming not to have seen me – creating the odd impression, only just short of hallucinatory, that he was optically, physically duplicated: a motionless, cold, studiedly detached figure thrusting me beyond the horizon of his vision, and another, full of paternal benevolence, hospitable, warm, obliging – he welcomed me to the Zafer Hermitage. Which was no longer, or not solely, a hermitage but a hotel – ugly, to be sure (who could deny it), but what can one do with these architects nowadays . . . Presumptuous, fanatical, unapproachable . . . Better, oh how much better, the master-builders of yore . . . For its ugliness, therefore, he was not to be blamed; for its comfort, to be praised a little . . . Architects! The two great swindles of the century were Architecture and Sociology. And Medicine was fast catching up with them, rivalling already the basest witch-craft . . . Then as though suddenly worried: 'You're not an architect, I hope, a sociologist or a doctor.'

'I'm a painter,' I said.

'A painter . . . Wait. I think I recognize you . . . Wait. Don't tell me your name . . . On television about three months ago — they showed how a painting is born, one of your paintings . . . Frankly you could have picked a nicer picture . . . But I suppose you did it on purpose — how an ugly painting is born into an ugly world, an unintelligent painting for those millions of unintelligent people who watch television.'

'You were there yourself, in front of a television set,' I said rather resentful.

'That's a compliment I don't deserve. I watch television too often to be able to say I'm totally uncontaminated by the leprosy of imbecility . . . Too often. And I'll finish by catching it. If I haven't already caught it . . . For I must confess that the contemplation of imbecility is my weakness, my sin . . . Pre-cisely: the contemplation . . . Giulio Cesare Vanini, who was burned at the stake, could see God's greatness in a clod of earth. Others see it in the firmament. I see it in imbecility. Nothing is deeper, more abysmal, more vertiginous, more incomprehensible. Only one shouldn't contemplate it too much . . . There, I've got it: you are . . .' and he said my name.

'I can't say I'm flattered by the process which led you to recall my name,' I said joking, but with some bitterness.

'No no. While I was talking about imbecility part of my mind was ticking away trying to catch up with your name. Quite an independent little mechanism, memory, at least mine is . . . So. You'd like to stay here today and tomorrow. It'll be an honour for us, but I'm afraid it won't be much of a pleasure for you. The whole hotel, however, apart from the few rooms which are occupied, is at your disposal.'

'But I'd have liked to stay on after tomorrow. I've heard that there are going to be spiritual exercises here.'

'Do you want to take part in them too?'

'Let's say that I'd like to exercise my spirituality by witnessing the spiritual exercises of others.'

'Idle curiosity in fact.'

'I do admit it.'

'Or worse: the satisfaction of catching other people doing what you consider, perhaps, unworthy of human beings — of laughing at them . . .'

'Maybe.'

'Well, one never can tell.'

'What?'

'Anything. You heard about our spiritual exercises and you felt like attending them . . . You think this impulse was motivated by the desire to have some fun, to make fun of others . . . But one never can tell what may come of a mere impulse — an act of freedom . . .'

'. . . to which then the links of causality become welded . . .'

He looked at me for the first time with some interest. 'Of course,' he said, 'the chain.'

He bowed imperceptibly. And disappeared.

I came down from my room when I heard the prolonged trill of a bell in the corridor – like the arrival of a train being announced in a station. I assumed that it was a sign that lunch was ready. And I wasn't mistaken.

The refectory was vast, crammed with circular and rectangular tables of which only two were set and occupied. Don Gaetano called me to his. My place was on his right. There were four other priests, among them the porter. The five women were at a table far removed from ours, but not so far that we couldn't hear their voices, their words, which merged within the circle they formed like water flowing from five spouts into a fountain. They stopped talking when Don Gaetano rose to say Grace. He included them in the blessing, but with just a hint of condescension and mockery in his strictly ceremonial gesture

– rather as one who, having eaten the meat, throws the bone to the dog. The women demurely crossed themselves, murmured Grace, crossed themselves again. And resumed their chatter. Don Gaetano sat down and, starting with mine, filled our glasses with wine, praising it as a connoisseur, but in those French terms now current among the uninformed. It was, he said, a local wine cultivated mid-way between mountain and sea. And he quoted in Greek the Greek poet who, according to him, had celebrated precisely this wine, from this locality. He spoke of nothing else. He drank with gusto and ate with distaste. And the fare was indeed distasteful – badly cooked, insipid. There was nothing for it but to add salt and pepper, which at least whetted our thirst for the truly excellent wine. At the end of the meal Don Gaetano apologized, telling me that the cook would arrive the next evening — eating would then be quite another matter.

No change at dinner. Nor the next day at lunch. Had it not been for my curiosity concerning the spiritual exercises and those who were to perform them I'd have left. Even though I greatly enjoyed Don Gaetano's conversation, whether he talked about wine or Arnobius, Saint Augustine, the Philosopher's Stone or Sartre.

Dinner on the second evening was much more palatable — even if only relatively so. The cook and his assistants had arrived late in the afternoon. They'd only been able to repair, amend. But the improvement sufficed to raise our spirits, as Don Gaetano observed. And he went on to pour scorn on those fools who pretend they don't care what they eat or are so naturally uncouth and ill-bred as really not to care. He spoke about French cookery – the only one which, justifiably, honoured a hero such as Vatel, who could be compared to Cato of Utica. For if the latter killed himself on account of a departed freedom, the former did so for a fish which failed to arrive. And his action had, before God, the same value, motivated as it was by the same passion: self-respect.

'But,' I objected, 'there's self-respect and self-respect, and even God can't compare a fish — which anyhow was only one of the many courses at the table of Louis XIV — to freedom.'

'And why not? Let's leave God out of this, since we know nothing more of his opinions than what is convenient to our salvation, and I think our desire for salvation probably influences our knowledge. So leaving God aside, and granted that self-respect is a valid choice, Vatel is a better example of it than Cato of Utica, for the fish ought to have arrived and did in fact arrive an hour after Vatel had killed himself . . . Whereas freedom . . . ?'

A discussion ensued which contributions from the four priests promptly confused and entangled. Don Gaetano and I let them fight it out — each of them having his say without paying the least attention to the others. And, dinner being over, we left them practically at each others' throats.

As we came out of the refectory Don Gaetano asked if I'd finally decided to stay and attend the spiritual exercises. I said that yes, I had. I thought he was pleased, roguishly. But brandishing his great white hand before my eyes he made a playful gesture of reproof and menace which implied that I was a wicked miscreant who hoped to surprise the true believer in his nest, in his stronghold, and that I'd have to pay for it. And so, leaving me with the vision of that hand still imprinted on my retina, he vanished. (Here I want to explain why, when describing Don Gaetano's departures, how he leaves or has left, I use the words 'vanish' or 'disappear' — and shall go on using them and perhaps others such as 'fade away', 'dissolve'. To do so I must resort to the memory of a game we played as children: we would draw on a sheet of paper a completely black figure with a single white spot in the middle, and we would stare fixedly at that white spot counting up to sixty, then shut our eyes or look up at the sky — and we still saw that figure, but now white, transparent. Something rather similar occurred with Don Gaetano: when he'd already gone his image seemed to linger on behind my closed eyelids or in space. So that it wasn't possible to perceive the precise, actual moment at which he left. Which was doubtless an after-effect of that kind of duplication I tried to describe earlier. The fact is that he seemed to establish a hypnotic sphere — but certain impressions are hard to communicate.)

70

Owing to a sort of restlessness which had troubled even my sleep, I got up at dawn on the great day. I didn't want to miss the arrival of those who were going to dedicate a whole week of their lives to those spiritual gymnastics without, however, mortifying their flesh since the famous cook had preceded them. I'd been over-impatient but I didn't regret it. I hadn't watched the dawn like that, from my bedroom window, for at least twenty years. In all that time I may have witnessed the odd one from a plane — but that's not the same. I stood for a while at the window enjoying the total and perfect harmony between nature and my senses. And I was seized by the desire to paint. A desire I promptly resisted for fear of distorting, of disrupting — in short, of failing. Because my desire was obviously superficial, more or less academic, in other words commonplace — the desire of someone who, not knowing how to paint, or knowing without being a real painter, sees a natural scene, a landscape, a particular disposition of objects in space and in light and says: 'that ought to be painted!' Which is precisely the most superficial and academic eulogy of nature and simultaneously the best way to debase and degrade painting which, for me at least, is about everything that ought not to be painted. Moreover it was a false desire, as I knew at the very moment I experienced it. I knew because I had cold feet; and ever since I'd read that quip of Voltaire's, that to paint well one must have warm feet, though he was referring to English painters (and I might have applied it satisfactorily to Bacon and Sutherland), I've taken it into account and kept a close check on it. The pictures I've painted with cold feet are the worst — which doesn't prevent them from being the most highly appreciated by critics and collectors. And I'd painted enough with cold feet really to want to paint one while I felt free, no longer bound to my profession, to the market, exhibitions, money, fame. Even if, alas, I owed my freedom to the fact that I'd got all these things already: a lot of fame, a lot of money, exhibitions galore, an ever rising market value, a profession which enabled me to spew out two or three paintings a day. With cold feet, of course. Those I painted when my feet were warm — not many nowadays — I kept for

71

myself. That is for a later and juster fame. But quite frankly I'm not particularly concerned with posthumous fame.

However I felt totally free. Even from painting. Or rather (since I'm on the subject this might be the moment to try and get things absolutely clear), this kind of flight, this illusion of freedom existed only to create a break, a breathing space before returning to painting with warm feet — according to the wise Voltairean precept. An impossible return. And I told myself as much in fits and starts — I'd go on painting a great many paintings with cold feet and a few, a very few with warm ones. But what goes on inside us is always horribly complicated. And we always delude ourselves most convincingly, or try to, when disillusionment appears most obvious and imminent.

So I stood a while at the window. Enjoying the total and perfect harmony etc. . . . Then I took a very hot bath, to warm my feet and thus put them out of my mind. And indeed I emerged from my bath invigorated. I shaved, brushed my hair, dressed. And went downstairs.

There was a lot of coming and going in the entrance hall. The staff was vastly increased. And also the priests — I counted seven new ones circulating busily. Too much confusion. And I went out on to the esplanade where an array of deck chairs had been set out — all vacant but distended and imprinted by the bodies they had cradled and appearing to have spontaneously broken out of the ranked order imposed on them to gather in groups. They recalled, on account too of the colours — natural wood and widely striped blue and red canvas — some early de Chirico. I entered into the picture — anyone looking out of one of the windows would have taken me for a mannequin abandoned on a chair (I experience the paintings of others more than my own — especially the work of those painters most different from me).

The esplanade, as I think I mentioned earlier, was vast. Besides the space occupied by the chairs there was ample parking and turning space for the many cars that would arrive. But it was nine before the first arrived.

The first four followed each other closely. As the first drew up in front of the hotel, Don Gaetano materialized on the doorstep. But perhaps he'd been there all the time. From the car a Bishop emerged. And a Bishop emerged from each of the three others. Once they were all gathered together I noticed that one of the three wore a red skull-cap instead of a lilac one. A Cardinal. I identified him, not very respectfully, I admit, thanks to a verse of Belli's: 'he took off the black and put on the red' — about a police patrol breaking into a brothel where the sergeant in command finds himself face to face with an austere looking priest who, removing his black skull-cap and replacing it with a red one, turns into a Cardinal. To the sergeant's intense embarrassment.

A Prince of the Church. And in consequence about a dozen motorcycles, with as many policemen one foot on the ground bestriding them, filled the esplanade with their din, drowning the voices of Cardinal, Bishops and Don Gaetano. These seemed to be exchanging greetings and jokes. Don Gaetano as usual in his cassock; the other four in dark grey suits, dark grey pectorals on which the silver crucifix stood out, and shiny starched collars. And skull-caps. None of the four seemed to have a distinct personality. Two looked like peasants and two like bureaucrats. The cardinal was a bureaucrat — of the relentless, hardboiled kind. Had they removed their skull-caps it was Don Gaetano at a guess who should have been the Cardinal — the others would have been parish priests, two from the city, two from the country. Despite his attitude of filial devotion, of gaiety and at times of mirth, Don Gaetano maintained a detachment, a dignity, an authority which aroused my deepest admiration. A Cardinal? He might have been the Pope himself.

The motorcyclists departed in a flurry of noise. In the unexpected silence I heard the Cardinal praise the beauty and magnificence of the Hotel. Don Gaetano, so it seemed to me, glanced in my direction with a wink of pitying irony — for the poor Cardinal who should have known, and didn't, what true beauty and magnificence were. Then he said: 'Eminence . . .' and led the little bunch of dignitaries into the hotel.

I'd been so intent on trying to hear what the Cardinal, the Bishops and Don Gaetano were saying that I hadn't noticed the arrival of the other cars. Nearly all with uniformed chauffeurs, therefore company or ministerial cars. Those who emerged must have been Ministers, Undersecretaries, General Directors, Chairmen, Vice-Presidents. Some however were driven by women. It didn't take me long to conclude that these were wives bringing their husbands so as to take back the car. One of them struck my fancy — not precisely beautiful (but I've never liked precisely beautiful women — I only married one and left her), but tall and shapely, intelligent looking, ironic, something unrestrained, impatient in her movements, her smile, the glint in her eye, as though she were about to burst into a great shout of freedom, a flurry, almost a flight of rapture. And while her husband opened the boot and took out his suitcases, she talked volubly. And her voice rang in my ears like an invitation, as if somehow in reminding her husband not to catch cold, not to over-eat, to put on his sweater in the evening and take his pills at mealtimes, she was telling me (since she had noticed and possibly identified me): I'm leaving this fool, this swine, this swindler, and for a week I'll be free, free, free . . . And while I was decoding her message she eyed me, amused, languid, defiant and determined, confirming it. Briefly, I was tempted to follow her or, more practically, to ask her for a lift into town, in front of her husband who would have benefited from a small dose of anxiety concerning his wife — if he was capable of such a thing — in view of the exercises he was about to undertake. But I watched her leave without moving — an absent-minded kiss to her husband, a last glance at me, her legs well exposed as she closed the car door. And indeed, someone was probably already waiting for her — at last a week all to ourselves . . . But for a while I cherished the illusion that for me she'd abandon anyone else.

The esplanade was now packed with cars and little piles of suitcases and bags. Porters came and went agitated and sweating. But they were obviously incapable of discerning the status of the arriving and waiting guests, so that some of these were hailing them and complaining in a tone of voice which implied: the cases you're taking before mine are those of my Vice-Chairman. Whereas I'm a Chairman and I should have precedence even if I arrived after him — or words to that effect. But apart from such isolated manifestations of bad temper directed at the porters, the atmosphere was one of easy, unreserved conviviality — exclamations of surprise, embraces, hand-shakes, bantering abuse. At the arrival of a Minister the jolly camaraderie subsided — there was a silent eddying towards his car like metal filings towards a magnet. Likewise for another three or four whom I failed to identify. But when Don Gaetano suddenly appeared that eddying which had converged upon the Minister and the other unidentified personalities was now directed towards him — but halting a good metre away from him in a semi-circle. And it seemed that in this semi-circle the order of precedence for kissing his hand was rigorously maintained. Don Gaetano acknowledged everyone, recalling with each some detail concerning his function or his family or the state of his health. And everyone was delighted to have been thus recognized and distinguished. But always, in what-ever Don Gaetano said or did there was an echo, a hint of mockery — which clearly no one in that herd gathered around him was capable of noticing. And I noticed, and this enchanted me. Because they seemed, that refined mockery, that subtle scorn, to bear witness to a kind of understanding, of complicity between him and me — and because he represented, if older and wiser and more accomplished, the ideal to which I aspired.

Suddenly the esplanade was empty, once again deserted and silent as in the morning. Or I suddenly became aware of this.

I re-entered the hotel. The porter-priests were now two. the one I'd seen on arriving and another who had been among the four I'd met in the refectory.

'What happens next?' I asked.

'The guests have gone to their rooms. In about half an hour they'll come down for mass. The Cardinal will celebrate it. Then Don Gaetano will speak.'

'In the chapel downstairs?'

'Yes, in the chapel downstairs.'

'May I attend?'

'I think so. Don Gaetano has nothing against your attending the spiritual exercises I gather, and since the exercises start

75

with this mass . . .'

I thanked him and wandered off. I was in two minds. Not because I might seem inquisitive — since I'd stayed on precisely out of inquisitiveness — but because I was afraid of being bored and of having to remain till the end out of politeness.

But I went. And was moderately bored. I hadn't attended mass for at least a quarter of a century (if I say a quarter of a century rather than twenty-five years it's all part of a desire to boast about growing old). And as it was the first time I heard it in Italian I indulged in reflections on the Church, its history, its fate. That is, on its past splendour, its squalid present, its inevitable end. For aesthetic reasons I was a believer. But my haphazard meditations derived from something more remote and obscure — something more dangerous. A basic unease or anxiety — as of someone setting out on a journey, or who has just set out and feels he's forgotten or mislaid some object but doesn't know exactly what. But if, at the risk of exaggerating, I was to confess fully my state of mind I'd say that I felt somewhat cheated and abandoned. That solid block to which I'd been, albeit resentfully, chained for years — that block of superstitions and fears, of intolerance, of Latin — was as friable and unreliable as a clod of earth. I still remembered (when I was ten I served mass) certain passages from the Latin. And I compared them with the Italian into which they'd been changed — precisely, changed, as one says of someone: how changed he is. 'By the mystery of this water and wine may we come to share in the divinity of Christ, who humbled himself to share in our humanity.' What insipid words! They conjured up a picture of those insipid people who add water to their wine at table. 'Deus, qui humanae substantiae dignitatem mirabiliter condidisti, et mirabilius reformasti: da nobis per hujus aquae et vini mysterium, ejus divinitatis esse consortes, qui humanitatis nostrae: Qui tecum vivit et regnet in unitate Spiritus Sancti Deus: per omnia saeculorum.' What remained henceforth of the significance of such words and, above or beyond their significance, of their mystery?

But that, I said to myself, is exactly what you wanted — to see the mystery dissipated, the squalid props of that imposing stage, to see the majestic illusion exposed as when we enter the theatre before Pirandello's *Six Characters* . . . Yet Pirandello's demystification of the theatre is a way of re-inventing and re-asserting it. So did I want the Church, by discarding mystification and deception, to re-invent and re-assert itself? No. I wanted it to end. And it had reached its end . . . And yet . . . The truth is that so many things which are part of us, which we believe are dead, linger on in a valley of sleep — neither pleasant nor Ariosto-like. And over their slumber reason must always keep watch. Or sometimes, just as an experiment perhaps, wake them up and let them out of the valley but only so that they may return subdued and impotent . . . And if the experiment fails? That's the point. At which, to be frank, I'd never found myself — since everything within and outside me had, for years, been pretence. My whole life was self-deception and deception. Only what one pays for is real, what one pays for in the currency of understanding and suffering. And I didn't pay for anything any more except through the bank. There wasn't an emotion, a belief, an idea for which I was required to do more than sign a cheque. Or a painting – since it's the signature that gives value to a painting, just like a cheque. (Some day I'll have an exhibition of canvases with nothing on them but my signature, fairly highly priced; and I'll suggest the following slogan to the dealer: Do-it-yourself — a famous painter has already signed it for you). Even the sufferings of others, the diseases, poverty, disasters which befall acquaintances or those I don't know but who turn to me for help, the wars in which whole populations perish, the oppressions under which they groan, a signature suffices to cancel their image and free me from guilt. And I'd freed myself thus from so many things. Too many for me not to feel at that moment cut off from reality, from life . . . The thought, half vexing and half ironic, crossed my mind that if I went on indulging such reflections and self-accusations I would in fact be performing my spiritual exercises. And I'd be the only one since all those who'd come to perform spiritual exercises seemed, and were, otherwise inclined. During mass they did nothing but whisper to their neighbours, wave and smile to those who were at a distance. They were on holiday. But a holiday rich in opportunities for the renewal of profitable relationships, for schemes to increase their power and wealth, to disrupt alliances and avenge betrayals.

'Mass is over. Go in peace.' But they mustn't go; therefore the bustling and shuffling which followed these words stopped short as soon as Don Gaetano appeared. Those who had been remiss were visibly ashamed. And upon their silent contrition Don Gaetano poured his reproach. His voice was drawling as if he were trying to repress a constantly recurring yawn. And without changing tone he passed from reproof to instructions — about the significance and the necessity, for each and all, of the exercises, of a scrupulous self-scrutiny, of a re-assessment of past and future actions, of a conclusive and anticipatory stock-taking. And, since all who were gathered there to exercise their spirit and renew their strength represented the Christian and Catholic world in the government of public affairs as well as in those things which concerned the welfare of the nation, it was imperative during the following week that they ask themselves, specifically, thoroughly: Have we rendered unto God that which is God's?

Here someone in front of me murmured to his neighbour: 'Obviously he wants to build another hotel.' Then glancing over his shoulder and fearing that I'd overheard, he smiled at me conspiratorially, assuming I was one of them, that I couldn't ignore what that saintly man — undoubtedly saintly but rather demanding — meant by 'rendering unto God'. Moreover Don Gaetano didn't specify the advantages of rendering unto God (understandably there was no mention of rendering unto Ceasar), but allowed the notion to penetrate each individual conscience and be translated, according to the influence and function of each, into concrete representations and figures.

'Now you can go,' Don Gaetano said at last, letting a residue of his initial reproof weigh on the first word.

All rose – in good order this time – and walked towards the exit. The Cardinal and the three Bishops had already vanished, perhaps into the sacristy. We were left, Don Gaetano and

78

myself, in the chapel which suddenly seemed larger. Don Gaetano, as usual appeared not to have seen me, but after a moment he began to talk to me. He knew why I had stayed behind.

'You haven't yet visited the chapel which is, in fact, the original Hermitage. As you see it was spared. It hasn't been tampered with since the seventeenth century . . . Zafer's Hermitage! A whole legend invented towards the end of last century by a local scholar . . . There existed some tradition or legend about a dark-skinned, white-bearded hermit. And a chemist from a nearby village found a name for him: Zafer. The chemist's mind possibly worked in the following manner: Zafu is a regional name; then there was Michele Amari's recently published translation of Solwan el Mota. Perhaps, who can tell, the chemist found the subject Christian — when certain passages are taken out of context the flame of Christianity may seem to flicker in the most unChristian texts . . . Zafu, Zafer — the latter so much more appealing: sapphire, saffron . . . And then there was this painting . . .' he pointed. I hadn't noticed it till then: a dark-skinned bearded saint with an open book before him and a devil, sanctimonious and mocking, whose red horns were like flayed flesh. But what struck me most forcibly in the devil was the fact that he wore glasses — black-rimmed pince-nez. Moreover the impression that I'd seen something of the sort without being able to remember when or where gave the bespectacled devil an aura of mystery and dread — as though I'd seen him in a dream or in a terrifying childhood vision. 'From this painting,' Don Gaetano went on, 'our chemist concocted a legend: the eyesight of Zafer the saint is failing; the devil offers him some lenses; but these lenses obviously possess a diabolical power — if the saint accepts them he will always, when he reads the Gospels or Saint Augustine or Saint Anselm, be reading the Koran instead. "Alas that the pure sign of Your syllables should change into contorted Cyrillic!"' The quotation amazed me: Don Gaetano had read the poet I consider to be the last Italian poet of the age of Italian poetry and knew some of the lines by heart! 'Kufic in this case, òr whatever the script of the Koran is called. Needless to say Zafer, aware of the deceit, refuses the gift. Indeed he totally ignores the devil . . . But this painting, as you doubtless know, is only a copy, and not a very skilled one, of the Manetti which is in Siena in the church of Saint Augustine. A curious painting none the less. Quite apart from the chemist's fantasies I would even say disturbing . . . A bespectacled devil? What Manetti wanted to represent is pretty obvious in relation to his own time, but today . . .'

'The same thing: any contrivance which enables us to see clearly can only be of the devil and from the devil. For you, for the Church.'

'A secular interpretation, of a traditional secularity — that of the confederacy imputed to Giordano Bruno and Francesco Ferrer . . . I on the other hand would say: all that which meddles with nature is of the devil and from the devil . . .'

'A sadistic interpretation.'

'But de Sade was a Christian,' said Don Gaetano turning from the painting to look at me in surprise — surprise that I didn't know, that no one had told me.

'If you say so . . .' with exaggerated irony.

'It isn't I who say so,' Don Gaetano said bluntly. He wandered about the chapel as if I hadn't been there. Then came back to the painting. Rather displeased with myself for the trivial irony of my 'if you say so', I tried to find something more subtly ironic to say. But Don Gaetano, having climbed the altar steps, had taken from an inner breast pocket of his cassock a pair of spectacles, placed them on his nose and, standing on tip-toe was leaning forward to examine the lower right hand corner of the picture. When he turned round to say: 'Here is the signature. Come and see,' I was seized with overpowering bewilderment — his glasses were an exact replica of the devil's. He didn't, or pretended not to, notice my only too obvious amazement — probably relishing it. While I tried to parry the blow as best I could — in case he had really enjoyed inflicting it — by assuming an expression that was meant to imply: old comedian, keep your spectacle trick for your flock of imbeciles. But he seemed equally oblivious of my transition from amazement to scorn. I came up to read the signature.

With some difficulty I deciphered b, u, t, a, s, u, o, c, o: Butasuoco.

'Buttafuoco,' Don Gaetano corrected. 'You didn't notice the second t and you mistook the f for an s. Nicolo Buttafuoco, a local artist. And according to another scholar of the century before last — no less fanciful than the chemist — the devil is a selfportrait, horns and all . . . One day as he was painting a Madonna, using a strumpet as model, he declared: "This Madonna will work miracles when horns have sprouted on my head". And lo and behold they sprouted. And that was the first of a long sequence of miracles that Madonna performed . . . Very apt, those horns, considering what a beastly painter he was.'

He removed his glasses and stored them in his breast pocket. And with the laboured indifference of someone who has made his point, of the cat who has eaten the canary: 'The name Buttafuoco is always associated, both in reality and in fiction, with something slightly sinister or at least suspect — this painter who represents himself as the devil; Boccaccio's Buttafuoco in the story of Andreuccio of Perugia . . . Delightful that study of Croce's on Boccaccio's tale — his discovery of a Buttafuoco in the Angevin registers among the Sicilian refugees . . .' And so he rambled on as, having taken my arm, we made our way to the refectory.

He asked me to his table once again. Instead of the four priests there were the Cardinal and the three Bishops. And two places had been added for the Minister and an industrialist. I felt ill at ease. Not because I'd never been at table with Ministers, industrialists and priests (not a day passes as a rule when I'm not sharing a meal with one or a whole collection), but because of the place and the occasion — a hotel run by priests, a gathering of Roman Catholics for the purpose of spiritual exercises. And if I felt surprised and out of place in that company, they seemed even more surprised at finding me there when Don Gaetano introduced me (impeccably introducing me to the four prelates, and the Minister and the industrialist to me). And maybe they assumed at first that I'd been converted. But when the Cardinal held out his hand to be kissed and I lowered it in the customary handshake they gave obvious signs of perplexity — directed at Don Gaetano. Questioning, preoccupied glances converged upon him. Don Gaetano explained that I was there by chance, out of curiosity, more or less by accident.

Since everything Don Gaetano did was for the best they were reassured. And at once they all felt the need to praise my paintings, the prelates those they'd seen in exhibitions or collections, the Minister and the industrialist those they possessed (and it turned out that they did have some, even some painted with warm feet). The conversation naturally proceeded to painting in general. And it became immediately apparent — despite their praise of my work— that for the four Churchmen the art of painting had been dead and buried for about a century — the last to have practised it being Nicolo Barabino, whose name brought to my mind the reproduction of his *Madonna of the Olive Trees* over my mother's bed which for years, probably ever since I was first able to hold a pencil, I'd copied: always miraculously according to my mother, according to me tolerably well, all things considered — while for the Minister and the industrialist it had never existed except, at a given stage of their lives and fortunes, as an investment and for its sale value. Thus they didn't see eye to eye with the priests — since the sale value of old paintings is variable for minor painters and incalculable, beyond any true or realistic appreciation, for major ones; whereas for contemporary artists, whether major or minor such prices are steady and rising steadily. Except that there were no major artists among our contemporaries, the Cardinal observed, adding without conviction: 'Apart from our friend here present, of course.' I protested without conviction, and reminded them of Guttuso. The Cardinal objected that he was far from being a major painter. Whereat Don Gaetano praised Guttuso's *Crucifixion* which had provoked a certain scandal thirty years ago but which now, he said, the Vatican Museum was hoping to acquire. One of the Bishops asked why there had been a scandal. 'Because the figures are all represented unclothed,'

Don Gaetano explained in a tone of mock surprise at those who, thirty years ago, had been shocked to see the scene of the crucifixion peopled with nudes. The prelates agreed that, when the intention was innocent, the fact of stripping Christ, the Virgin and the afflicted was a wholly innocent enterprise. And indeed far greater sacrileges were perpetrated in our day against that sublime tragedy. We were about to hear a list of contemporary sacrileges when one of the Bishops reverted to the subject of Guttuso suggesting that he was a Communist.

'But who isn't?' said Don Gaetano. Then parodying: '*For we can't not claim to be Communists.*'

It wasn't clear whether he was serious or joking. However his words were greeted by all, and even by me, with mixed approval. And silence descended.

I broke it, reluctantly but with forced frivolity, asking in a playful, mocking voice what they thought of Paul VI's reinstatement of the Devil.

'Oh the Devil,' the Cardinal snorted ironically. And his irony, I perceived later, was not directed only at me, the enquirer.

'I wonder, with all the respect, all the filial devotion due to the Holy Father,' said the Minister, 'whether this was the moment to tackle the problem of the Devil.' And he glanced at me defiantly, taking me as witness of his open-mindedness, his daring before a Cardinal, three Bishops and a priest famed for his cunning, erudition and power.

'It is the moment,' Don Gaetano asserted, stressing the is.

There ensued what I vaguely perceived as a flutter of re-adjustment in the minds of the four prelates and the two devotees. As when we hear that a newly erected building is collapsing, that cracks are appearing. Some cracks were appearing in their minds.

'I don't say it isn't the moment,' said the Cardinal. 'I'd say rather the manner . . . I don't know . . . perhaps one could have . . .' And he stopped, prudently letting anyone else who was willing expose himself to Don Gaetano's thunderbolts. But no less prudently the three Bishops and the two devotees evaded the theological controversy (disappointing me slightly) and began to consider Paul VI's statements on the Devil as a purely bureaucratic matter, as a ministerial circular, and the Pope as a minister whose decrees, more or less awkward, more or less obscure, are the concern of the cabinet, some of whose members are devoted to the minister but incapable, some capable and not devoted and some neither capable nor devoted.

'And his health? The Pope's health?' enquired the industrialist.

'Popes,' said Don Gaetano, 'are always in good health. One might even say that not only do they die in good health but of good health. I speak, it goes without saying, of mental health,' turning to the industrialist, 'since your enquiry, obviously innocent of implications, referred to that . . . Other indispositions, other infirmities don't count.'

'Indeed,' I said. 'It's never occurred that a Pope has gone out of his mind through senility or artereosclerosis. I mean it's never been known to occur.'

'It's never occurred. Exactly,' said the Cardinal.

'It's never been known to occur,' I repeated.

'What isn't known doesn't occur,' said Don Gaetano.

'I'd say that some things may not be known but occur,' I replied.

'Yes. I agree. But remember that we are talking about the Church, the Pope . . .' said Don Gaetano, 'a force without force, a power without power, a reality without reality. What anywhere else would be mere appearance to be hidden or disguised, in the Church and in those who represent it is the interpretation, the visible manifestation of the invisible. That is to say everything . . . Which needn't stop us from digging up, if we are so inclined, the oddities, whether innate or the effect of senility, of certain Popes . . . Of Pius II for instance, whose delightful *Commentari* when examined attentively . . . The very fact of writing the story of one's life when one is a Pope . . . An occupation better suited to a soldier of fortune than to a Pope . . .'

Cardinal and Bishops stiffened, protested. But it emerged that they hadn't read the *Commentari*, whereas Don Gaetano was able to support his theory by quoting entire passages. 'I

84

would suggest,' he added, 'that at a certain point, the point at which he began to dictate the *Commentari*, Pius II was no longer able to contain the pleasure he derived from his ascension to the pontificate which he owed more to his own than to the Holy Spirit. The irresistible need to proclaim: look at me here on the throne of Saint Peter, still Aeneas Silvius, the same Aeneas Silvius who wrote *De duobus amantibus*! I've made it! I've had you! . . . A Stendhalian hero *avant la lettre*.' Then to appease the Cardinal who, embarrassed, was trying to call him to order by clearing his throat disapprovingly: 'But he was a great Pope, Eminence. Very great and saintly . . . And I've got an idea: since he died in the night of 14th August 1464 I'll talk about Pius II at the end of the second session of exercises, which will fall precisely on the anniversary of that date.'

'A very good idea,' the Cardinal said. But coldly.

'Excellent,' mumbled the Minister chewing hard. And he pointed, waving his fork like a sprinkler of Holy Water, at his plate. He was signifying that the stuffed guinea-fowl was very much to his taste. And I now realize that while reporting our conversation I've failed to give an account of the liveliness of the hall and the quality of the 'refreshments' (as our midday and evening meals were described). The menu — a printed folder on thick paper with the Devil tempting the Saint reproduced on the cover — was exceedingly abundant. And it materialized before us, excellent, as the Minister had intimated, in quality as well as quantity. Everything had suddenly changed in Zafer's Hotel. The refectory was packed, the cook was surpassing himself, the service was prompt and attentive. It was carried out, apart from a dozen or so waiters, by a team of young girls whose belonging to some Third Order or other didn't preclude a certain amount of coy flirtatiousness. Further details: on each table a tastefully arranged bouquet exploded; the five women had been spirited away; it was the Cardinal who said Grace. And here I must add that I felt like a dog in Church or, to be true to my principles, I should say like a man in dog-kennels when everybody stood up, crossed himself, prayed, sat down again. But I have to confess that I didn't remain seated, as I had planned, when they all stood up.

Leaving the refectory I intercepted the porter-priest, the one who'd been reading *Peanuts*, to ask where the five women had vanished to.

'What a question! They keep to their rooms,' he replied, mysterious, almost evasive.

In the afternoon the Cardinal opened the exercise session. He spoke for over an hour. I listened absentmindedly — but less so than his flock. He quoted the Bible, especially Exodus, discussing the theological movement — new if I'm not mistaken — of hope. As far as I was able to gather, what this movement called hope was despair. Not a single reference to the Gospels and only one or two to Christ.

When the Cardinal turned the last of the pages from which he'd been reading a restrained sigh of relief arose from all sides and merged into a single puff like that of a deflated balloon. At the end of his speech there was applause. The Cardinal silenced them with a gesture. And when they had subsided Don Gaetano told the audience to go to their rooms and meditate on His Eminence's words for an hour in solitude. I surmised from exchanges I overhead among the departing flock that they were otherwise inclined. There was talk of books to be read, stories to be told, letters to be written, telephone calls that had to be made. Indicating a short, bespectacled, ascetic looking man, a stranger beside me as we left observed: 'There's someone who's not at a loss for something to do in his room.' I asked who he was and what he'd do in his room.

'What, don't you know him? He's . . .' mentioning a famous name.

'Of course. I thought I recognized him . . . And what is there for him to do?'

He waved his hand to signify marvels, unheard of delights, while his face lit up with voluptuous malice, greed, envy. And suddenly suspicious, he left me.

On the esplanade there were only two men talking earnestly. They were discussing ways and means. Don Gaetano, coming out behind me, caught them in the act. He pointed an accusing finger: 'My friends! I'm surprised at you. Still here discussing our common misfortunes? Go to your rooms and meditate on His Eminence's words.'

Like children caught raiding the larder, the two separated. One after the other they slipped into the hotel. Don Gaetano smiled and came towards me: 'I'm prepared to wager that you'll meditate better on the words of His Eminence than the whole lot of them.'

'You do me too much credit,' I said. 'I'm meditating, it's true, but on the doubtless spiteful remark someone made to me as I was coming out of the chapel. He pointed out . . .' (I named the man who'd been pointed out to me) 'saying something like: "there's a man who knows what to do in his room". I was wondering what he meant, exactly.'

'A woman, of course.'

'A woman he keeps in his room?'

'Not quite. The woman has a room of her own.'

'One of the five. I see.'

'One of the five, yes. And all five are here for the same purpose. Though naturally not for the same man.'

'And you tolerate . . . ?'

'My friend, I tolerate everything. I admit and permit.'

'But I mean, the spiritual exercises . . .'

'It seems to me that you have more faith in them than I have. That you take them literally or according to their original Ignatian significance . . . And furthermore I believe that laicism, that which makes you define yourselves as lay, is only another form of exaggerated respect for the Church, for us priests. You see the Church, and ourselves, as aspiring to a sort of perfection which you prefer to keep at a safe distance. Our response can only be to invite you to join us in trying to be imperfect like us . . . However I'll try to see things in your perspective, that is to see the spiritual exercises as mortification . . . Well, these five gentlemen have wives, children, electors, opponents, friends and enemies who blackmail them, friends and enemies who watch their every step, listen in on their phone calls . . . Each of them has got himself a mistress as is the custom. And during the whole year they dream of their

87

week here of spiritual exercises — and they end up doing them
. . . They send their women on ahead. Making them understand, naturally, that I wouldn't have accepted them had they
not been vouched for by their protectors as women with
shattered nerves, in need of peace and quiet and a break from
their private worries, their misfortunes, in a suitably religious
atmosphere. I pretend I don't understand, don't know. And I
accept them. Because I do know that their imaginary week of
love will turn into a week in hell . . . The fool you overheard
thinks they are experiencing the joys and ravishments of love.
Do you know what they're doing instead, those five adulterers,
those five sinners. They're bickering. Bickering for no reason
at all or for some insignificant reason, as a kind of self-castigation
— precisely because they feel guilty of adultery, of sin . . . If
you were to go and listen behind those five doors — as some
people are probably doing at this very moment — you'd hear
them bickering, and not just like any ordinary married couple,
but with far more venom, more ruthlessness . . . Believe me,
the best way to make love is to do it spontaneously, fleetingly
as one does with a prostitute . . .'

'So you then . . .'

'It's such a simple thing, to make love . . . That's what love
is — there is no other between men and women . . . It's like
being thirsty and drinking. There's nothing simpler than being
thirsty and drinking. Being appeased by drinking, by having
drunk. Not to be thirsty any more. Simplicity itself. But think
of what would have happened if we'd invested water, thirst,
drinking (if creation and evolution had taken a different turn)
with all the emotions, considerations, rituals, sanctions and
prohibitions with which we've invested love! There'd be
nothing more extraordinary, more prodigious than drinking
when one was thirsty . . . And as to prostitutes — ask yourself
whether the most satisfactory drinks you've had in your life
weren't from a fountain at a street corner, a roadside spring in
the country . . .'

'That's not new, about thirst and drinking.'

'Not new but revolutionary. Lenin, you may recall, raised
the question of the glass, refused to drink from a glass someone

else had used before him. Somewhat reactionary, don't you think?'

'Puritanical. I'd say puritanical. Like all revolutionaries.'

'Yes. If he'd said I always drink from the same glass . . .'

'I agree. But don't you think you're even more reactionary when you postulate the existence of prostitutes?'

'But I'm as reactionary as I'm revolutionary.'

'And glasses present no problem for you?' With a hint of malice.

'Stop. Don't be coarse. Try to forget all the spiteful, vulgar literature about the clergy in which every Italian, even the practising Catholic is steeped. Be more subtle, more serious . . . I can say of myself what a medieval chronicler said of Arrigo VII: "He was chaste in body, and chastity must have pervaded his whole being". It's chastity that makes me simplify what we are in the habit of calling love. And it's non-chastity that makes you complicate it. Of course, I acknowledge it: chastity is terrifying. But only when we first make the choice and come to grips with it . . . What happens afterwards is something like what happens — and here you'll follow me — to art for those who practise it: the limits and restrictions of expression become the form, no longer limits and restrictions. Similarly chastity is the most sublime form self-respect can achieve. It's like turning life into an art.'

'I can't live,' I said, 'if I'm not in love — together with all the complications that involves. Not always with the same woman, of course. One goes out of my life and another comes in. And sometimes the second comes in before the first has gone.'

'But I wager it's always the same woman. I mean her personality if not her actual appearance.

I thought for a moment. 'Maybe you'd win your bet,' I said.

'You see! You suffer from a more or less widespread, more or less common affliction . . . We cease to be children at puberty but most of us manage to go on being children in the sphere of eroticism to which puberty gives access. Let me explain: the most important discovery child psychologists have made — among their many important discoveries — is what they call something like "the law of repetition of the same thing or its substitute", I can't remember the precise term. On the other hand it was so easy to perceive . . . A child wants to be told the same story, prefers the same toy, repeats the same game. Even when he's no longer a child. Donjuanism is simply an extension of this law beyond puberty, through into youth, into old age. You've gone from youth to old age skipping the stage of maturity, precisely because maturity for those who suffer from this disease, doesn't exist. Donjuanism is an extension of immaturity right up to second-childhood — which is after all an apt precursor — to death . . . You may have noticed that all Don Juans end up in second-childhood.'

'I'll kill myself just in time. Admitting that I really am afflicted with Donjuanism.'

'You are. And you won't kill yourself just in time — for the simple reason that you won't be able to perceive the boundary line, the frontier.'

'Don't you think you're using the age-old weapons of Catholic sexophobia just now against me? Except that you predict second childhood instead of Hell.'

'You're very much mistaken. There never was such a thing as Catholic sexophobia. In the past there was only embellishment and refinement. Maybe today, in the age of permissiveness, a tendency towards sexophobia can be anticipated . . . As to predicting, that is to say threatening, I'm not threatening you with anything. I made an observation. You can make it yourself if you take the trouble to look. Men who run after women, first one woman and then another or two or three at a time, you have surely known. Try to recall the last years of their lives.' And he left me to the pursuit of this distressing enquiry.

Punctually after an hour the esplanade was again swarming with guests. They'd meditated, that was obvious. They were anxious to communicate to each other the results of their meditations — offers in figures and figures as offers, spicy anecdotes about hated friends and dear enemies, flattery, con-

90

descending appraisals. And the odd well-worn dirty joke. For the most part they were whispering in pairs. And I remembered the seminary rule of *nunquam duo* which ought to be enforced in all Catholic gatherings. It was easy to guess that the pair on my right was plotting against the pair on my left and vice versa, and likewise every pair against every other pair. So that the esplanade was like a loom on which was stretched a solid weft of conspiracies, of betrayals, the shuttle passing from hand to hand.

I drifted from pair to pair, from group to group, catching a word, a snatch of conversation, a whole conversation — whispered, sometimes interrupted or hesitant, sometimes resolute. On the whole everybody seemed to be discussing the midday meal and the one that would follow in a couple of hours — one man's lack of appetite, another's hunger; there were those who ate everything, didn't feel like eating anything, wanted to but couldn't, had to be forced to eat, had to stop eating too much, there's a limit to what one can eat, and so on and so forth. I realized that they were talking figuratively and, perfecting the image, I saw them reeling in an avalanche of decomposing victuals.

I strolled off towards the wood. And came back to the hotel to find everybody in the refectory.

Don Gaetano beckoned me to his table. My usual place. The Cardinal and the Bishops were no longer there. Other men, whom Don Gaetano introduced, occupied their seats. Their names and professions were not unfamiliar. I announced my intention of leaving the next day.

I didn't join in the conversation despite the variety of topics it involved. Indeed I didn't even listen except when Don Gaetano spoke. His contributions were always brief and to the point — quotations dropped with cold authority, jokes, witticisms. Mostly for my benefit, since his usually expressionless gaze, distant, vague, when focused on me seemed to light up with curiosity and speculation concerning my silence. As though he were intimating that he shared my impatience but wanted to show me how they ought to be treated. But I was out of sorts even with him.

When the meal was over the guests went outside. They appeared to be gathering around Don Gaetano, not casually but as if for some pre-established, compulsory purpose. And curiosity dispelled my bad temper.

They formed a circle. At a given moment, perhaps when they assumed that everyone was present, the circle broke up and they disposed themselves in ranks. Don Gaetano, who had been at the hub of the circle, was now in the middle of the first rank. Thus arrayed, they remained for a while motionless and silent. Then Don Gaetano's voice intoned: 'In the name of the Father, of the Son and of the Holy Ghost, Amen.' And the ranks began to advance. As I've said, the esplanade was vast. And it seemed vaster because nearly all the lights had been extinguished. The ranks marched from the hotel entrance to the opposite side. When they got there they seemed to disintegrate in disorder and struggle to reassemble while the Paternoster was chanted in chorus. Once reassembled they returned towards the hotel. And in the light which streamed through the door and the ground-floor windows I saw that the foremost rank, though Don Gaetano was still in its centre, didn't include the same people as at the start. And I realized that the exercise was more orderly than it had seemed from a distance — shortly before the right-about-turn Don Gaetano would stop and allow his rank and those behind it to divide and advance on either side of his stationary figure, closing up again so that at the moment when the right-about-turn was actually effected he was in the middle of the last rank which, after they turned would be the first. Doubtless some of these gentlemen got muddled — but the chanting of the Rosary proceeded undisturbed.

Someone came and sat down beside me. I took no notice. But when I heard him unmistakably chuckle and sneer I turned to look. He was in shirt-sleeves, a towel round his neck, another in his hands with which he dried his face and head. He said: 'I come here every summer so as not to miss this spectacle, even though they pay badly. Look at them,' he sniggered mockingly. Then hurriedly, as at the cinema when one doesn't want to lose the thread of the story, miss the hero's entry: 'I'm the cook.' And he was absorbed once again by the spectacle, chuckling from time to time.

And not without cause. That to-ing and fro-ing in the half dark esplanade, not as for a quiet stroll but urgently, like people afraid of the dark and hurrying to get back to the light (by the hotel entrance — and indeed their steps seemed to drag there as though to linger a while before resuming their march towards the darker regions); those voices raised in the Paternoster, the Ave Maria, the Gloria, slightly terrified, hysterical, Don Gaetano's voice following theirs, clear, cold, and from this voice such expressions as: 'the hidden message', 'the secret of salvation', 'the ancient serpent', 'the sword that will transfix the soul' assumed an entirely physical reality, ceased to be metaphors and became events that were about to take place, that were taking place in that spot on the frontiers of the world, on the frontiers of Hell which was Zafer's Hotel. And at that moment even those who, like myself, like the cook, saw these people as abjectly deceived and grotesque, realized that there was something real — real terror, real distress — in their march through the dark, their chanting of prayers — something really akin to a spiritual exercise. Almost as if they were in despair, experienced despair in some circle of Hell and were on the verge of a metamorphosis. So that what came to mind was the thieves' pit in Dante's Inferno.

'Did you enjoy our Rosary performance?' Don Gaetano asked me the next day.

'Very much.'

'I knew you'd like it.'

'A pity there were only two of us to enjoy it — the cook and myself.'

'Ah, the cook . . . Yes I know, he's an *aficionado*. An intelligent chap, one can tell from his cooking. But a rabid anticlericalist, of the old school. I don't think he's a communist. A republican perhaps, or a socialist . . . But you're mistaken when you say there were only the two of you to enjoy it. I was enjoying it myself.

93

'May I ask a question?'

'By all means.'

'What sort of a priest are you?'

'A priest like all the other priests.'

'No. I certainly wouldn't say that.'

'Do you know a lot of priests?'

'I've known a few. As a boy, a young man. In a small town. Two or three good ones, nine or ten bad. The good were those who didn't meddle in other people's affairs. They were not calculating and mean when they had to marry, bury or christen someone. They were responsible for the odd embellishment, or rather damage to their church. They didn't provoke any gossip. The bad ones were those who were grasping and miserly. Who let their church go to ruin. Who set wives against their husbands during confession. Who were surrounded by Ursulines, Daughters of Mary and moneyed bigots. But, good or bad, all were equally ignorant.'

'I see your problem. You don't know whether to count me among the good or the bad . . . Well, I'm very bad.'

'No. That's not my problem.'

'Oh yes it is . . . And you'd already have solved it by placing me among the bad if it weren't for the fact that I don't happen to be ignorant . . . "J'ai lu tous les livres . . ." But you can ignore that fact. I'm a very bad priest who, unlike the other bad ones you've known, has read a great many books . . . Actually, I'd like to present you with a little paradox, just to make it clear that if I count myself among the bad priests it's not out of humility but out of conviction: good priests are the bad ones. The Church owes its survival — more than its survival, its triumph throughout the centuries — to its bad rather than to its good priests . . . It's behind the image of imperfection that the image of perfection resides — the priest who transgresses saintliness or, in his way of life, makes utter havoc of it, in fact confirms, exalts, serves it . . . But this is a very commonplace truth. I could perhaps refine or elaborate it.'

'So the greatest Pope was Alexander VI.'

'That too is commonplace — a witticism I might expect, if

94

you'll pardon me, from the cook. But I'll follow it up on your terms. Alexander VI was, *malgré lui*, a great Pope. Were I asked to choose between Pius X and Alexander VI . . .'

'You'd choose Alexander VI.'

'Precisely. But we are, remember, in the realm of paradox. If we emerge from it, I can further tell you that the greatness of the Church, its trans-humanity, resides in its consubstantiation of a kind of absolute historicity — the inevitable and strict necessity, the unchanging utility of every internal event in relation to the world, of every individual who pertains to it and bears witness to it, of every unit of its hierarchy, of every mutation and succession . . .'

'You're a fanatic.'

'Do you think I could not be a fanatic in my position? If, that is, for you a fanatic is someone with convictions . . . But my convictions — and this is something you didn't suspect — are as corrosive as your doubts . . . Moreover, let's return to paradox if paradox is the form of truth you find most acceptable.'

'No let's avoid it. Tell me, on the contrary, as simply and concisely as possible what the Church is.'

'Well, a good priest would say that it is the community summoned by God. I who am a bad priest say: it's a raft, a raft of the Medusa perhaps, but a raft none the less.'

'I remember Gericault's painting but I can't recall exactly what happened on that raft, although some years ago I read a whole book about it. Something horrendous, proverbially horrendous . . . Was anyone saved on that raft?'

'Fifteen out of one hundred and forty-nine — maybe too many . . . No no. I'm not talking about the raft of the Medusa. I'm talking about that of the Church. Ten is a rather high percentage.'

'How about what those fifteen did to save themselves?'

'I don't really care. I mean I don't care since the raft of the Medusa is a metaphor, for me, of the Church.'

'I'd rather die straight away in the shipwreck.'

'No you wouldn't. You're swimming towards the raft right now. Because the shipwreck has already occurred . . .' He smiled, half amused. 'Hadn't you noticed?'

He was gone. Reflecting on the raft of the Medusa, trying to recall what had happened on it, I strolled towards my car. I couldn't remember the details but I experienced the same horror as when I'd read about them. Cannibalism probably. 'This is my body. This is my blood'. *Totem and Taboo* — my first encounter with Freud, an important revelation, a blinding flash. Later one learns that important revelations derive from a less sensational, steadier light, almost imperceptibly . . . But no, I was not swimming towards the raft. Nor had the ship-wreck already occurred. Life was still, for me, a secure vessel with its mast upright — how to translate the 'steamer balançant ta mâture' of that poem of Mallarmé's from which Don Gaetano had earlier quoted the half line: 'J'ai lu tous les livres'? Completing it in my head: 'La chair est triste, hélas! et j'ai lu tous les livres', I dispelled the disturbing image of shipwreck and raft.

I drove into town. A furnace. But I plunged into it with a certain relish — as if by accepting the heat, the scorching summer I opposed Don Gaetano and his Hermitage-Hotel with its coolness, its delightful breezes.

I got back in the early afternoon, but only to go and doze in the woods. At least that was my intention. But I ended up in the glade where the women were sun-bathing. And this time in their company. A delightful afternoon. Though I didn't play the game too earnestly, especially with the one who was keenest (but she was keenest because I'd been unable to dis-guise the fact that she was the one I preferred), since the next day, I had now definitely decided, I'd be going away. And if I was staying another night in that dreadful hotel it was only because I wanted to attend once again the Rosary act. I was fascinated by it, like the cook.

But to the chain of the causal and the casual another link was being welded.

Dinner proceeded as usual. Four other guests had replaced the four who, the previous day, had replaced the Cardinal and the Bishops. I assumed that Don Gaetano, while maintaining the

Minister and the industrialist as permanent fixtures, varied each day, according to I don't know what principle of precedence or preference, their four table companions. He introduced them. Not unfamiliar names, neither was mine to them. One of the four, Chairman of an important national firm, was an ex-Senator who had recently resigned to take up this post. An angular foxy face. Far from uninformed in matters of Patristics and scholasticism. And all through the meal there was, between him and Don Gaetano, an exchange of quotations like a game of ping-pong. I was myself not uninterested in Origen, Erasmus and Pseudo-Dionysus, but in a purely unorthodox manner. Rather like Borges, simply trying to understand.

As on the previous evening, after dinner we all flocked out on to the esplanade. I went and sat by the cook who was already at his post. 'You've become addicted too,' he said by way of a greeting.

'Yes I have. It's a fascinating spectacle.'

'Priceless. I'm well placed to say so since, to a certain extent, I pay for it. And one of these days I'll pay dearly — I'll catch my death of cold, I will.' He rubbed himself carefully with the towel he was holding — face, neck, head, ears. 'You've no idea how hot a kitchen can get. It's hell. And I come out into the open air without taking proper precautions, what with being too busy in there and not wanting to miss any of the show . . . But it's worth it. Christ, it's worth it. To see all these sons of bitches going up and down chanting the Rosary . . .'

'The Church,' I said, 'provides entertainment even for non-believers.'

'Maybe. As far as I'm concerned, bugger the Church!'

'Then how did you get involved with this priest's hotel?'

'By chance. Or rather thanks to a friend's tricks. He told me: I'm not well. Go and replace me for a couple of days. But really he'd got himself another better-paid job. When I found out, I wanted to chuck in the towel. But Don Gaetano . . . Besides there was that show . . . But I told Don Gaetano, I told him straight: one of these days I'll put a kilo of rat-poison in the soup, and goodbye to you.'

97

'And Don Gaetano?'

'D'you know what he said, that old son of a bitch?' There was veneration and devotion in his voice. 'He said: My son, let me know in good time so that I can skip the soup that day. That's the sort of man he is . . . Oh, but it's starting.' And he settled back in his chair.

Indeed it was starting. The ranks advanced as Don Gaetano's voice intoned: 'In the name of the Father, and of the Son and of the Holy Ghost.'

'The Angel of the Lord . . .'

'Our Father which art in Heaven . . .'

'Hail Mary . . .'

'Glory be to the Father . . .'

'Our Father . . .'

'Hail Mary . . .'

'Glory be to the Father . . .'

'Salve Regina . . .'

Now from Don Gaetano, now from the chorus the prayers rose in the dark night — and everything, the voices, the significance of those words, the absurd to-ing and fro-ing like caged animals, their hovering and lingering in the half light and their quicker terrified scurrying towards the dark, everything seemed part of some raising of spirits, some invocation mingled with that hint of hoax and extravagance non-believers always detect in spiritualist meetings.

'Holy Mary . . .'

'Holy Mother of God . . .'

'Holy Virgin of virgins . . .'

'Mother of Christ . . .'

'Mother of Divine Grace . . .'

'Mother most pure . . .'

A memory surfaced, not of the Latin words themselves, but of how those words were pronounced by the women who, in winter round the hearth, in summer out in the yard, gathered to recite the Rosary during my childhood. And the memory added an extra touch of the ludicrous, especially when I recalled their distortion of certain words which trivialized their significance and made nonsense of the whole thing.

98

'Tower of Ivory . . .'

'House of Gold . . .'

'Ark of the Covenant . . .'

'Gate of Paradise . . .'

And Don Gaetano had only just uttered these words, and the words 'Pray for us all' were being intoned by the chorus, when there was a noise like a bottle being uncorked.

The ranks had reached the part of the esplanade furthest from the hotel entrance and from where the cook and I were seated. They had barely reconstituted themselves after the right-about-turn, and there, between the 'Gate of Paradise' and the 'Pray for us all' the noise made them stop and falter for a split second, then immediately disperse and scatter.

Don Gaetano stood still. And behind him, some ten or fifteen metres away, a pale smudge, a bundle.

It took me about thirty seconds to identify the bundle as the prostrate body of a man. Precisely the time it took Don Gaetano, who had remained perfectly motionless facing the hotel, to turn round and walk towards the fallen man. I saw him bend down and touch the body. The cook and I rose simultaneously and ran to the spot. We arrived as Don Gaetano, one knee on the ground, his right hand raised was saying: 'Ego ti absolvo in nomine Patris, Filii et Spiritus Sancti.' He looked at us, then got up. 'He's dead,' he said.

It was the ex-Senator, Chairman of the big national firm who over dinner had played the quotation game with Don Gaetano. In death his face had lost some of its foxiness and become almost fragile, as though fashioned from a brittle substance, and painfully serious. I looked at him in the flickering flame of my cigarette lighter. Then I looked at Don Gaetano and the cook. Totally impassive the priest. And the cook was sweating more copiously than at his oven.

Those who had fled now returned. And in their converging upon us there was eagerness as well as reluctance, the desire to know and to see, with the dread of what they were about to see and to know. They were asking each other and, as they drew near, they asked us: 'Who is it? What's happened? How did it happen?' with contained excitement. Till they were all gathered in a tight circle round us and the body. I extricated myself followed by the cook. Don Gaetano said: 'We must call the police,' and cautioning us on no account to touch the body he too extricated himself from the circle and walked with long deliberate strides towards the hotel.

We returned to our seats. Oddly enough I'd resumed the attitude of a spectator — as though aware that the crime was only another instalment in a serial and that its purpose was simply to up-date that improbable chanting of the Rosary and add to it an extra thrill. But the cook was terribly worried. 'It's lucky,' he said shakily, 'that we were together.'

'Why? Do you think they'll suspect us?'

'One never can tell . . . Someone, they'll have to suspect. And they're not likely to look for him among that lot. Could any of them be suspected of murdering a comrade? And while reciting the Holy Rosary?'

'But it can only have been one of them.'

'That's what you say. And what I say. But the police won't begin to think of one of them till they've made quite sure neither the waiters, scullery-boys, local peasants, you or I had any reason on earth to despatch that gentleman . . . Made sure, I repeat. And you'll see how . . . Though maybe they'll show some consideration for you.'

'Especially,' I teased, 'since I never expressed any desire to poison them.'

'Don't remind me of that. You may be joking but if the police get to hear of it they won't let go of me. I know them. Oh don't I know them!'

'You've had dealings with the police?'

'I have. Not for anything I did. For something that was done to me. As victim of a robbery. Robbed of my wallet by a stranger to whom I gave a lift. I made a statement and guess what they went and imagined?'

'Rigged robbery.'

'Exactly. They grilled me for half a day. Married? Yes. Any extra-marital relationship? No. Gambling? Never. Not even the National Lottery? Not even the National Lottery. Debts? Not a penny. How much was there in your wallet? About a hundred thousand lire. Precisely? I don't know. Impossible. Very possible indeed . . . And so on and so forth on this point till, exasperated, I said to the Inspector: "Tell me how much you've got in your wallet precisely." He thought for a minute — because he was taken aback. Then he said dryly: "Thirty seven thousand five hundred". And I, innocently: "Let's see". What a rumpus that created! They sent for my wife and gave her to understand that I was keeping another woman. Oh I went through hell, I can tell you. As the victim of a robbery. Just think what it'll be if they hear what I said . . . But Don Gaetano's a friend. He won't let on. And if someone else does I'm sure he'll stand up for me.'

'Of course,' I said, sorry I'd teased him.

Don Gaetano came back. He stood on the porch, clapped his hands to attract attention, then said in a loud voice:

'All of you. Come here.'

Slowly they all drew near. Don Gaetano said: 'The police are coming. I was advised on no account to move the body and to keep as far from it as possible. And that no one leave the hotel, of course, or go to bed. For he'd have to come down again . . . All of you sit down on this side, then. And try to recall anything you may have seen or heard at the time of the shot or just before. The clearer and briefer your answers are the sooner we'll get moving.' He clapped his hands again but turning towards the inside of the hotel where the waiters were gathered: 'Bring a sheet to cover the corpse. And turn on the lights.'

The lights came on in three waves — a blinding crescendo. At the far end of the esplanade the dead body, foreshortened in my angle of vision, seemed more dead than before. Then two waiters, dropping a sheet over it, turned it into a little mound of snow. The night was suddenly filled with a dense ballet of midges, with geckos streaking across the walls towards the glaring lamps. It was as though a horror, till then unperceived, had been unexpectedly exposed. Even the pervasive silence seemed related to that in which the geckos darted. (I've always had a phobia about geckos. And those who maintain that geckos have their use in a natural order since they feed on midges which destroy the vegetation, must acknowledge an element of disorder, if not in the existence of geckos, at least in that of midges — that a better order would ensue from the non-existence of destructive midges and of geckos to devour them.)

At a certain point the Minister's voice — remarkably tentative considering the arrogance of his words — was raised:

'Don Gaetano, did you tell the police that it's we who are here?'

'Who are we?' Don Gaetano said coldly, deliberately.

'Why us, all of us . . . Me, our friends . . .' The Minister was suddenly embarrassed.

'I told them you were here, yes,' Don Gaetano said. But as much as to say, yes I had to admit that I keep bad company. Which endeared him to me. It also endeared him to the cook who nudged me.

The Minister wasn't happy. The auditorium — for we were disposed like an auditorium around the corpse — settled back into silence. Then Don Gaetano said: 'I don't want even to consider the possibility of its being one of you . . .' And everybody all of a sudden began to consider such a possibility. That it might be one of them. Except of course the murderer. They looked at each other as if each of them might suddenly perceive in his neighbour the man who had killed. 'I think,' Don Gaetano added, 'that someone may have fired from the wood, perhaps as a joke.'

'Why, the old son of a . . .' whispered the cook while a chorus of approval rose up from the auditorium.

It hadn't yet subsided when the police noisily arrived.

'Very good,' said the Inspector at a glance — all of us on one side, the corpse left well on its own just as he'd recommended. He went up to Don Gaetano and shook hands with him.

'My dear Inspector,' said Don Gaetano.

'What a disaster,' said the Inspector. And he walked over to the corpse followed by Don Gaetano. Instinctively I got up and went over too. And the cook after me.

The Inspector lifted the sheet, looked, sighed, let it drop. 'Who is it?' he asked Don Gaetano.

'The Chairman of Furas, the Onorevole Michelozzi . . . Elected Senator in the last elections. But he resigned to become Chairman of Furas. An excellent person. Cultured, conscientious, honest.'

'I don't doubt it,' the Inspector said. But with just a hint of irony. As much as to say, even if I wanted to doubt I couldn't.

'Indeed,' said Don Gaetano reflecting the hint like a beam in a mirror and redirecting it at the Inspector implying, as it were, there's nothing you can do, my friend, you'll have to comply.

'The Hotel staff . . .?' asked the Inspector.

The cook gave me a dig in the ribs.

'All above board,' Don Gaetano replied. 'Not a thing to say against any of them.'

'And here in the neighbourhood . . . ? I mean, a peasant who might have some grudge against you, against the Hotel . . . Something of the sort . . .?'

'No one has a grudge against me,' Don Gaetano said. pained. 'And the peasants, those that are left, have benefited by the Hotel. They sell chickens from their hen-houses, or eggs — which they buy in town — cheeses, vegetables . . . People come here and go away thinking they're bringing home healthy country butter and other foodstuffs . . .'

'But some fanatic perhaps . . .'

'You're referring to the fuss that occurred when I incorporated the Hermitage into the Hotel . . . No, no. That's all over. Major principles vanish before major profits and minor fanaticisms before minor ones.'

'But there has to be a motive . . . Or rather, apart from the motive, someone must have fired. Because, as to shooting — he was shot, wasn't he?' His gaze included me and the cook as he awaited confirmation.

'So it would seem,' said Don Gaetano.

'And who shot him?'

'That, my dear Inspector, I believe it's up to the police to find out.'

'Yes, yes,' sighed the Inspector. 'It's up to the police, of course it's up to the police . . . But the police, when the shot was fired, weren't here . . .'

'Whereas we, on the other hand, were . . . But believe me, we are no further advanced than the police who weren't. At least all of those who were assembled here reciting the Rosary.'

The cook nudged me again.

'Apart from the murderer,' I said.

Don Gaetano looked at me — as usual as if he didn't see me. And with profound amazement as though my remark had somehow precipitated him into the depths of sorrow or raised him to the heights of hope: 'Then you think one of us, one of those saying the Rosary with me,' stressing 'with me', 'was the murderer?'

'I'm sorry, but that's what I think.'

'And why?'

'Why do I think so? First of all because, being myself an amateur shot, I have, so to speak, a good ear — I heard the shot as dull, deadened, as if the weapon were pressed against the target, the body. And I'm ready to bet that he was shot in the back, that his coat, in the spot where he was struck, is probably singed . . .'

'We can't check straight away. We'll have to wait for the Public Prosecutor and the doctor,' said the Inspector.

'And then?' Don Gaetano asked with the condescension of an examiner who has already decided to fail the candidate.

'And then — but this is mere conjecture — I think that if it had been an outsider shooting from a distance, from the wood, there would have been more than one shot — two or three, for the fun of firing into a crowd . . .'

'And what if someone lurking at the edge of the wood hunting rabbits or hares had inadvertently let off a shot?'

'Rabbits and hares,' I explained, 'are hunted by moonlight and there's no moon. They are hunted with a rifle and what I heard was a pistol shot.'

'You heard it, the pistol shot. I heard a noise that could have been a pistol shot or a rifle shot or the uncorking of a champagne bottle,' Don Gaetano observed.

'He wasn't killed with a champagne cork,' said the cook.

I was surprised that Don Gaetano didn't respond to the cook's irony. He said: 'Of course. Yes . . .' and vanished.

The Public Prosecutor arrived and after him the doctor. I had seen the Prosecutor before but I couldn't remember where or when. It was like when you meet someone you'd known stout and he's thin, or thin and he's stout. But the Prosecutor was neither stout nor thin. When he caught sight of me after what in their jargon is called 'the identification of the corpse', I noticed that in his mind the same process was taking place as in mine — by the fixity of his gaze, the way he rubbed his chin. And when at a given point he heard the cook call me by name — with that expression one assumes after finding the answer to a problem for which another is still groping — he said to me: 'Remember? First B, 1941 . . . or 42?'

'41 . . . Yes of course I remember — Schembri.'

'Scalambri,' he rectified.

'Yes, yes. Scalambri . . .'

'After more than thirty years . . . And I think I'd have recognized you at once anywhere else. But here . . .'

'You're surprised to find me here. And quite frankly so am I to be here . . .'

Very friendly he took me by the arm: 'How are things with you then? Tell me . . .'

I felt acutely ill at ease. I've always tried to avoid meeting both old schoolmates and youthful flames again. Meeting them, that is, after a long time. And now to the discomfort of having met one after thirty years was added that of the place, the circumstances, my old schoolmate's specific role and the familiarity with which he treated me. The fact that we'd spent some months in the same classroom was not all that significant as regards our affinities, our feelings. Only two of my school-mates had played any part in my school years — one I'd continued to see and one I'd never seen again. We were all three at the bottom of the class. But we read a great many books which had nothing to do with the syllabus, we went to

105

the cinema together, discussed our amorous successes and failures. Scalambri, as far as I remembered, was among the good pupils, those who were unbeatable at Greek or Italian translations into Latin — this last being the task we considered the most odious and senseless of impositions.

I had nothing to say to him about myself. I'd have liked to discuss instead the crime. But as soon as I touched on the subject he became evasive, unconcerned, non-committal — either because his profession required it or because his interest in the case, the problem, was really too intricately involved with his annoyance at having been summoned at that hour, to this gathering of priests and politicians where caution, prudence and meticulousness in his investigations were of the essence. Though judging by what he was like at school these must always have been considerable. However, our conversation was interrupted by the Minister. Scalambri recognized him. He let go of my arm and forgot me.

The Minister was exaggeratedly obsequious. And no less so my former schoolmate.

'My dear Chief Inspector,' said the Minister after an exchange of spurious courtesies. 'You will want, I assume, to hear from each of us his impressions — since impressions, I believe, are all we are in a position to report . . . But, as you see, we are very numerous . . . So would it not be possible, if I may be so bold as to suggest, to postpone till tomorrow, at whatever time you think best . . .'

'But of course, of course,' Scalambri promptly agreed.

'Thank you,' said the Minister. He stood for a minute, thoughtful, examining Scalambri's face as though it were a map on which he sought to discover a familiar name, a country he knew. Then he sighed deeply concluding his sigh with the words: 'What a mess!'

'I know nothing about it,' Scalambri said warily. 'Except for what the Inspector has told me — the victim's identity, the shot . . .'

'Such an honest, upright, reliable man . . .'

'Exemplary,' Scalambri added.

'Truly exemplary,' the Minister said — as if without his

'truly' that exemplariness might almost have seemed incredible or ironic.

'Precisely for that reason,' Scalambri specified, 'the case has every chance of becoming, as you rightly observed, a mess . . . How on earth are we to — I don't say find — but even imagine a motive?'

'Yes, yes, you're right. One can neither find nor imagine . . . Dare I suggest there was none?'

'There always is, Sir, always — futile, crazy, imperceptible to the untrained eye, but it's always there.'

'Correct,' the Minister conceded. 'Correct. But futile, crazy . . . He can only have been the victim of insanity, that poor, dear Michelozzi.' And the name came out in a sob.

'A man beyond reproach,' said Scalambri. But only to show the Minister that he shared his grief.

'Beyond reproach,' the Minister echoed. And there came to my mind another distant echo — that of the cat in Collodi's great book who always repeats the fox's last word. He continued: 'And to think that he resigned his Parliamentary mandate to take on the Chairmanship of Funas.'

'A noble sacrifice,' said Scalambri.

I'd had the impression from the start that I was listening to a Ionesco play. But enough is enough. And since the two were as engrossed in each other as a couple of lovers on a bench in front of Saint Germain, entwined in the midst of the rush-hour crush, I left discreetly.

I found the cook still anxious. I reassured him. I wished him good night. And I went up to my room where till three in the morning I could still hear the murmur of voices rising from time to time to an angry shout from the police.

I woke at nine. And with the impression that I'd dreamt the events of the previous night. But their reality was confirmed beyond a doubt when I opened my window. There were policemen on the esplanade, grey-green police cars and, where Michelozzi had fallen, a sinister outline drawn in chalk with a reddish stain at the place of the lungs.

None of the guests was about. Still in their rooms, perhaps, like me — or at their exercises.

When I came out of my room the silent corridors reminded me of a convent. But as I approached the lift, the staircase, I heard an indistinct continuous murmur, profound, almost subterranean.

They were in the entrance hall, packed. Zigzagging clusters coiled and closely stacked one against the other and all together. It was like a Steinberg drawing.

Mingling with the coils I learnt that the Public Prosecutor was carrying out the interrogations in Don Gaetano's study. He'd asked all those who were in Michelozzi's row when, after the shot, the latter had fallen, to come forward first. No one had come. The Prosecutor had expressed, in measured terms, his disapproval. And everyone agreed with him — disapproving: how could anyone not recall whether the unfortunate Michelozzi had been at his side or not? But in fact even those who must have been beside him were asking that question, so either they really didn't remember or they preferred not to be involved. Apart, that is, from the person who had fired and who had every reason to lie low. However the Prosecutor had then begun to summon them in alphabetical order. And there, awaiting their turn, were even those whose initial was Z who, if all went well, couldn't possibly be summoned before late in the evening.

Scalambri had been top of the form. He'd probably come out top in the Law School finals. But as interrogator he was certainly not a master mind. He should have started with me and the cook who had been sitting apart, and then proceeded by reconstituting the ranks, appealing to the memory of each one. As it was he'd created a state of panic and everybody was, literally, evasive.

I approached the door of Don Gaetano's study. A policeman on guard thought to intercept me saying: 'I'm sorry but you must wait for your turn.' I'd had no intention of entering the room. But his intervention made me decide otherwise. I took out my sketch-pad and sketched, in the manner of Steinberg, the ranks of the faithful. Underneath I scribbled: 'The ranks should be reconstituted.' And I gave the page to the policeman. 'I'll give it to him when he calls me,' the policeman assured me.

He was called a few minutes later. And three people emerged then from Don Gaetano's study — Scalambri, the policeman and the man who had just been interrogated. The latter dived into the crowd as though to escape from Scalambri, to merge with the rest, to vanish. The policeman pointed me out to Scalambri but he was already coming towards me brandishing the piece of paper with the drawing on it and shouting: 'You must sign it!' The request made everyone stop talking. They turned towards Scalambri expecting, probably, to see that what he was holding was a cheque. They looked surprised to discover that it was a sketch. I was surprised but for a different reason. Although I was inured to, even sick of being asked for my signature — usually by waiters for the merest doodle I'd automatically traced on a paper napkin or in the margin of a newspaper while impatiently waiting for some woman — Scalambri's request really verged on the grotesque, the insane. I felt like answering as Picasso once answered a girl who wanted him to sign a sketch he'd just given her: 'Oh no, my dear, this sketch is worth nothing but my signature is worth a million francs.' But I refrained. I said: 'No no. It's nothing, hardly my own — more like Steinberg, or Flora. I'll draw you one with all the appropriate rites and rituals.' Scalambri was amused by the expression: 'With all the rites and rituals! I see you are conforming to the circumstances.' Then: 'But seriously, promise.' 'I promise.' 'Today?' 'Today.' Reassured but just to be on the safe side pocketing the sketch, he asked: 'Do you mean we should arrange this lot as they were last night for the chanting of the Rosary?'

'Exactly.'

'You're right. Questioning them one by one doesn't get us anywhere. I've already tried six or seven — they can hardly remember their own names.' He turned to the policeman and sent him to fetch the Inspector. Then he clapped his hands to attract the guests' attention. Having obtained it: 'Gentlemen, I've seen that it's quite useless to try and interrogate you one by one. I shall therefore try to jog the memory of some of you in the hope that the rest will be encouraged or obliged to remember . . . You are requested to go outside and arrange yourselves as you were last night when you began to recite the Rosary.' And he uttered the sacred word with such ambiguity as to signify to them: 'I'm one of you,' while displaying for my benefit all his private scorn for the Rosary and those who recited it.

Some agitation ensued, the odd outburst of indirect protest which Scalambri pretended not to hear. But the Inspector, who had arrived in the meantime, began, together with the policemen, to see that the order was carried out. And they scurried about like sheepdogs herding a flock into its pen.

Everybody was outside at last. And all gathered round Don Gaetano who had unexpectedly appeared. Just like the previous evening, except that the change from circle into ranks may have been less spontaneous and more laboured. 'I don't suppose,' Scalambri whispered, 'that you were there with them. So you are the only one who can help.'

'Not the only one. The cook was sitting beside me.'

'Bring the cook,' Scalambri shouted.

They brought him. Convulsed with fear. So that I regretted having got him involved.

Scalambri on the front porch was like a conductor on his podium. 'You two,' to the cook and me, 'go and sit where you were last night . . . Don Gaetano,' less imperative, 'try to help me please — who was in the front rank with you when you started?

'His Excellency the Minister most certainly. And certainly too poor Michelozzi . . .'

'Michelozzi was in the front rank then. At least something we're finally sure of,' Scalambri said. 'And then . . . try to recall who else was in the front row . . . How many were there in the front row?' turning to me and the cook.

'Seven, eight . . .' I said.

'Seven, eight . . .' the cook repeated.

'Seven, eight . . .' repeated Scalambri. And entreating: 'Don Gaetano, and you too, Eccellenza, try to recall . . .'

'Let me see. I was on Don Gaetano's right,' said the Minister.

110

'And on my right was . . . Who was on my right?'

'I was,' someone shouted and raised his hand.

'Good, Write it down Inspector. Professor Del Popolo on the right of his Excellency. And on your right Professor Del Popolo?'

'On my right . . . Dear me, who was on my right?'

'I was.'

'Write: the Onorevole Frangipane on Professor Del Popolo's right . . . And on your right Onorevole Frangipane?'

'On my right there was Ingegnere Lodovisi,' the Onorevole replied.

'Of course,' said Lodovisi coming forward with his hand raised.

'And on your right Ingegnere Lodovisi?'

'On my right there was no one.' Almost relieved.

'On Don Gaetano's left,' Scalambri said with a sigh that expressed both his own longsuffering and his grief for the deceased whose name he was about to pronounce, 'there was then poor Michelozzi. But who was on the left of Michelozzi?'

A dreadful silence descended. Then, trembling, a voice was raised, hesitant, a hand: 'Perhaps . . . I don't know . . . I think . . .'

'Avvocato Voltrano,' Scalambri announced.

'Yes but . . .' said Voltrano.

'Were you there or were you not?'

'Yes I was there. But . . .'

'But?' Scalambri was now firm, determined.

'Nothing. Just an impression.'

'What impression?'

'The impression, in fact, of not having had him beside me all the time.'

'How is that?' Scalambri was growing fierce.

Voltrano seemed to find the determination of innocence: It's just that I've got this impression . . . of not having had him beside me right through.'

'Ah,' said Scalambri, suspicious, ironic.

'Naturally,' I found myself intervening. Without wanting to.

111

Scalambri glared at me. Had it not been for our former familiarity and the sketch I'd promised him he'd certainly have had me evicted. He controlled himself and was content with a: 'Naturally what?'

I rose, came up to him, drew him aside: 'I say naturally because as always there are two possibilities: either Voltrano did Michelozzi in and, fearing that sooner or later we might discover that he was on his left, he's trying to find a loophole, pretending he thinks somebody may have crept between him and Michelozzi. Or Voltrano's innocent, is telling the truth — someone manoeuvred in such a way as to steal up from his own rank till he was, at the precise moment when they'd reached the darkest spot, next to Michelozzi . . . Find someone from another rank who has the same impression as Voltrano — that at a given moment he wasn't next to the person he was next to at the start — and you'll have the murderer at your mercy.'

What I said was too commonsensical for Scalambri. Insofar as he was top of the form. 'But you,' he said with a pitying smile, 'you're addicted to detective novels, or perhaps you even write them . . .'

'I write them and publish them under a pseudonym,' I retorted with a seriousness that baffled him.

'But this isn't a thriller,' he said returning to his investigation. But from then on he followed the course I'd suggested.

. . .

The whole morning went by like this: who was on your right, who on your left. Whether on your right or on your left did everyone always have the same person. Apart from four, five including Voltrano, they all asserted that no change, no substitution had occurred on their right or on their left. Of course no one could swear to it on the Gospels — the transition from light to darkness, their intense (so they said) involvement in the Rosary, the fact that they couldn't even consider a crime in their midst and that it should occur precisely during their humble, peaceful prayers (Leo XIII's encyclical *Supremi*

Apostolatus quoted by the Minister) which were a distinctive prerogative of the Christian faith — because of all these things their minds had retained little or nothing of what the Public Prosecutor now required them to remember. As to the five who expressed some doubts regarding the persistence at their sides of those who were undoubtedly there when the recitation of the Rosary began, they were all in the same position as Voltrano: a fleeting impression and no more. Nor were they able or willing to reveal who at a given moment they had found next to them instead of the person with whom they had first set out.

Scalambri was furious. Proceeding as I had suggested, he'd managed after four hours to reconstruct the ranks (which, it emerged, formed a trapezium rather than a square). He'd found five people who vaguely recalled not always having had the same person beside them on the right or on the left. But the inquest was no further advanced than at the start, nor could one foresee the possibility of any evidence whatsoever coming to light, were it only enough to dismiss the case. He was so furious that, in front of Don Gaetano and the Minister, he railed against the religion and the religious observances of those gentlemen whose memories so obstinately failed them.

The Minister chafed, seething with indignation. Don Gaetano on the other hand was quite unruffled. He didn't say a word. Only at lunch after prayers and Grace, pressed by Scalambri who was on his left — myself on his right — he began to thaw. But avoiding with incomparable expertise any reference to the crime whenever Scalambri tried to lead up to it. He knew, or at least suspected, something — of that I was convinced. And so was Scalambri who whispered in my ear as we left the table: 'If that confounded priest would only talk . . .' with an angry growl like a mastiff that can't get its teeth into the prey.

'What are we going to do, sir?' the Inspector then came over to enquire.

'What do you want us to do?' Scalambri snapped. 'We stay here as guests in Don Gaetano's Hotel. Whether something emerges or nothing emerges, there's nothing else we can do but stay here and observe, enquire.'

113

'Can I speak?' the Inspector asked with a significant glance at me.

'Speak.'

'I'd arrest the lot, including Don Gaetano.'

'And so would I, my dear Inspector, so would I . . .' Thoughtfully.

'Anyhow,' the Inspector persisted, 'they're all in the same position as the chap who, hearing that he'd been condemned exclaimed: "For all the things I've done you never condemned me. Are you going to condemn me for what I haven't done?" Don't you think?'

'I do, my dear Inspector, I do . . .' And passing from thoughtfulness to self-pity and then suddenly pulling himself together: 'Oh but this wine! It's treacherous . . .' And he went off unsteadily leaving me with the Inspector.

'And him as well,' muttered the Inspector watching Scalambri exit. Him as well to be arrested or him as well complicating matters by drinking more than he should in circumstances which required lucidity and decisiveness. Then suddenly cautious — on account of the familiarity he'd observed between Scalambri and me — he tried to rectify, to mitigate: 'I mean him as well, like me. That wine has had some effect on me too . . . And as everybody knows, where there are priests there's a good cellar.'

'Don Gaetano's a connoisseur,' I said to draw him out. 'A true connoisseur.'

'And not only of wine — of everything.'

'Even of crimes?'

'Of crimes in general I wouldn't know. Though at confession he's seen many an open sewer . . . But you know, I'd wager my last penny . . . in short I'd be prepared to bet whatever you like that, as far as this crime is concerned he's guessed something, he knows something.'

'I'm convinced of it too.'

The Inspector became inquisitorial: 'Do you know him well?'

'I don't believe anyone knows him well.'

'True,' he agreed ruefully.

'He's an extraordinary man.'

'Extraordinary.'

'Formidable.'

'Formidable.'

'Very intelligent.'

'Very intelligent, yes. Formidable, extraordinary . . . But you see, if I had him at my mercy for twenty-four hours, to question in my own way, as I know how to question, Don Gaetano'd puke out his soul, if he has a soul . . . And for heaven's sake don't go and imagine any kind of cruelty, of torture . . . I'd just get him off his pedestal. I'd just show him that for me he's no better than a poultry thief, an addict caught with his three grams of heroin in his pocket . . . When a man who thinks he's the cat's whiskers comes into a police station and is told to take off his shoe-laces and his belt, he goes to pieces, my friend, he goes to pieces in a way you wouldn't believe possible.'

'Even Don Gaetano?'

'Even Don Gaetano. Even the Pope. And God Almighty . . . Try to imagine the scene: a police station, squalid like my own, with that typical smell Gadda has immortalized and which you can't help smelling when you hear the word police (I smell it myself despite all the years I've been subjected to it). Behind the desk, the Inspector who doesn't get up, doesn't give the slightest sign of acknowledgement — let alone deference. The sergeant, standing there, indifferent, or even scornful says: "Mister Montini, take off your shoelaces and your belt . . ." It's the end, my friend, the end.'

'I'd rather imagine the scene with God Almighty instead of the Pope.'

'As you please, as you please . . .' He left smiling to return a second later, worried: 'Look here, for God's sake — I've been letting off steam with you in private because I know you think like me.'

With an understanding smile I asked playfully: 'And what do we think, you and I?'

'We think . . .' he made a semicircular gesture with his hand — scything, beheading. And, all smiles again, went off.

115

Actually it was years since I'd thought there was any call for scything, beheading. And that such a thought or desire now extinguished in me should flourish so luxuriantly in a police inspector, even if only in secret, was something I'd never have expected. But I'd lost touch with such a lot of things, so many changes, so many innovations had passed me by unnoticed. And not only me. All those I met every day were in the same position. Ministers, deputies, professors, artists, business men, industrialists — what we tend to call the ruling class. And what, in fact, does it rule? A cobweb suspended in the void, its own fragile cobweb. Even if the threads are gold.

Sadly reflecting on this cobweb, the golden thread by which I hung, which a movement in the branches, a breeze might destroy at any minute (and I stopped to contemplate a shimmering, silver cobweb — not gold this one — stretched between the branches of a hazel; displaced one of the twigs to which it was attached, bent it toward me then let it go like a catapult — and watched the silver threads snap and the spiders scurry hither and thither like mad), I'd strolled toward the clearing where, in the past, the women had sunbathed. They were not there. I continued for another hundred metres or so and suddenly I came upon Don Gaetano who, sitting on a circular stone — the grindstone of some ancient oil-press or mill — was staring at me but as usual appearing not to see me. I approached. And more unpleasant and offensive than the impression of not being seen was that of his not wanting to see me. I felt as a result rebellious, the urge to be unpleasant and offensive myself.

'Has someone told you in confession that he committed the crime or bore false witness?'

'Sit down,' Don Gaetano said making room for me beside him on the millstone. Deflated, I tried to resist. I declaimed: 'None can tell by whom he's loved when happy on the wheel he rests.' But I sat down on the cool stone which seemed to exude dampness.

The silence was immense, made more immense, almost

tangible by the distant horizon of voices, motorcars, barking dogs. We're testing each other at the silence game, I thought to myself. For the countryside, that countryside, brought back memories of my childhood, of its games and, among these that game we used to play when we'd had our fill of exercise and which consisted in not talking, not laughing, keeping our eyes shut. But I knew that I'd be the loser. Indeed, after a while I asked: 'What do you think of the way my friend Scalambri's handling the inquest?'

'Oh, so he's a friend of yours?'

'Not really. I said it as a manner of speaking. We were at school together. I hadn't seen him for years. I had no idea he'd become Chief Inspector . . . Do you think he'll find something?'

'Do you?'

'How can he be expected to, poor devil, investigating into this kind of congregation?'

'Don't say poor devil. Of poor devils there is only one, Satan . . . And you're very much mistaken in believing that this is a kind of congregation. It's a nest of vipers.'

'Are they biting each other?'

'Hadn't you noticed?'

'I haven't a sharp enough eye to notice . . . At any rate they won't bite each other for poor Scalambri's benefit.'

'Who knows? It might be enough to fish them out of their nest and see who is most bitten.'

'And the one who has the fewest bites is the murderer, I suppose?'

'Suppose what you please.'

'And you?'

'Me what?'

'You won't do anything to help Scalambri solve the problem?'

'The problem is Scalambri's. It cannot and must not be mine.'

'But justice, Don Gaetano, expiation . . .'

'No.' Firmly. Then as though extracting his words from some far remoteness: 'You see, the belief that Christ wanted to put an end to sin is the oldest and commonest error in Christendom.

117

"God doesn't exist, therefore nothing is permitted." No one has ever seriously tried to reverse those famous words — such an easy, obvious, simple operation: "God exists, therefore everything is permitted." No one except Christ, I mean. And Christianity in its true essence is precisely that: that everything is permitted. Crime, suffering, death . . . Do you think they'd be possible if God didn't exist?'

'The triumph of evil then . . .'

'Not evil. Not the triumph of evil. We should discard such words. All words . . . And yet, we have nothing but words . . . We should penetrate the inexpressible without feeling the need to express it . . . But you, I gather, are not interested in the inexpressible. So let's come down to earth . . . Let's come down then to the old accusations, the old defences. To Tertullian for instance, who desperately as well as vainly tried to defend the Christians when they were accused of not participating in public life. "We too frequent the forums, the market places, the baths, the shops, the warehouses, the inns and all your meeting places. With you we inhabit the world." Very true. Except that for us the world is something quite different. It is the edge of the abyss, inside us and outside us, the abyss that invokes the abyss. The horror that invokes horror. Therefore you justifiably fear us. And Tertullian was wrong to ask you not to fear us, to try and reassure you. But he was right to assume that to the extent that you condemn us, God absolves us.'

'Who you?'

'You who believe the world's governed by the forum. And the forum by God, even if you call God by other names.'

'And to come down a step further. You, what would you say? That the crime which has been committed here, among your guests, the fact that one of your guests has been murdered and that another, the murderer, will most probably never atone for it, is no concern of yours? Is that what you'd say?'

'I might even say that.'

'Why?'

'Because there's a part of me which is still exposed, still bare, still vulnerable, if you like.'

118

'And it isn't the better part I gather.'

'There you go again with your distinctions and divisions — better, worse; just, unjust; black, white. Whereas there's really only a fall, a long fall as in dreams . . .' The last word lingered as though absorbed by the air, the trees, by me — so that when I noticed I was alone, sitting on that circular stone, bemused, I felt as if I'd been overcome by sleep for a moment and had dreamt. Perhaps for more than a moment.

I stood up and walked towards the hotel. And already before reaching it, from the noises, from the voices, I knew that something had happened.

What had happened was that Voltrano, taking flight, so they said, from the window of his eighth floor room had crash landed on a pile of bricks and tiles. At the back of the hotel, on the kitchen side. The cook, dozing on a deck-chair, had been roused by the crash. At first he'd seen nothing since from his chair the pile wasn't entirely visible. Then noticing that some bricks were being dislodged, he'd got up and seen the pyjama-clad figure, face downwards, still jerking. He'd given such a shout that everybody, even those whose rooms were on the other side, had heard. Scalambri had heard him too, through a thick mist of wine-induced sleep. And he was there now, on the kitchen side, very wide awake, very angry, vociferating.

Pale, his teeth chattering, the cook was surrounded by cronies and scullery-boys one of whom continually handed him a mug of wine. The cook, who was shaking so violently he had to hold it with both hands, would take a quick sip and pass it back. When the Inspector noticed he protested that they were making the chap drunk when it was essential that he remain clear-headed. The cook cursed under his breath — the Madonna, all the Saints: 'Clear-headed! And why should it be clear, my head? What have I to do with it? I'm woken up by a crash and I see a fellow in pyjamas jerking on those bricks like a lizard that's been shot through the head by a catapult. That's all.' He stretched out his hand for the mug and withdrew it instantly cursing again. 'And I can't even drink a sip of wine!'

119

The young long-haired priest came up to me: 'He's upset, poor chap. I've never heard him swear.' To exonerate the cook and the hotel. Then: 'Poor Signor Voltrano. Did you know him?'

'No.'

'A person of great distinction — Sacra Rota, annulment of marriages. But he'd recently taken to politics, like that, on the side. But with great skill, great authority . . . Poor man. Every year when he came he'd insist: "Please, a room on the top floor". And we always complied.

'This year too,' I observed.

'Yes yes. This year too.' And he shuddered.

'Don't have any qualms about having complied. He'd have died even if he'd been on the seventh or the sixth floor. Even if he'd had a room on the first floor — without the business of throwing him out of the window.'

'Do you think he was murdered?'

'Don't you?'

'Good God! Another!'

'Once you've started a thing it's just a matter of carrying on.'

'But a crime . . .'

'Precisely with crimes. It's hard to stop.'

'So you think there'll be more?'

'No, no. Here and now everything may be concluded. It's hard to stop, I mean, till the blunders have been repaired, the accidents, the loose ends left hanging after the first one. Till the imponderables which may crop up later have been tidied away by a further crime. And so on . . . This, naturally, in crimes whose author has taken every precaution to achieve impunity. And since there's always a margin where the imponderable, the fortuitous, chance, play a fatal part . . . And that was the case here. If this morning Signor Voltrano hadn't expressed a doubt, the suspicion that perhaps during the ritual of the Rosary Michelozzi wasn't at his side all the time, he would still be alive.'

'So you think that on account of what he said this morning . . .

'Or of what he didn't say.'

120

The Inspector must have had invisible antennae attached to his ears since, distant as he was and apparently wholly concerned with solving the problem of how Voltrano could have fallen from his window on to the pile of bricks which was at least ten metres away (a policeman was at the window of Voltrano's room letting down a stone at the end of a string), he overheard the last observation and shouted to me: 'Quite right. For what he didn't say . . . And he was thrown from the terrace, as you can see, not out of the window of his room.'

'And what does that mean?' asked the priest.

'That means, my dear friend, that Voltrano went up on to the terrace for a purpose. That he went because he had an appointment up there with the person who killed him.'

'Please Inspector. Keep your insights for yourself and for me,' Scalambri intervened harshly.

'I'm sorry, sir. I'm sorry. But it was such a coincidence . . . Your friend here suggesting an hypothesis at the very moment when, it having already occurred to me, I was checking it . . . Physics isn't a matter of opinion. See for yourself . . .' He pointed to the policeman at the window holding one end of the string at the other end of which the stone, about a metre off the ground, oscillated nowhere near the pile of bricks.

'But what you don't know is that my friend writes thrillers,' Scalambri said, mollified, playful. 'He's not only the famous painter we all know . . . And by the way, that sketch? As Horace said: *Promissio boni viri est obligatio* . . .' Or was it only Trilussa who attributed it to "Orazio" because he needed a rhyme for *obligatio*?'

'Don't ask me. Me and Latin, you know . . .'

'Whereas I loved it, I loved it.' He sighed sadly at the fate which had turned him from Cicero and Lucretius and led him to inquests among the powerful, the untrustworthy, which involved two mysterious crimes. 'Well? That sketch?'

'You'll have it by this evening or tomorrow. Anyhow as things now stand, from here neither you nor I can get away.'

'We're like a convoy stuck in the mud.'

'Sir,' the Inspector broke in, 'would you care to come up to the terrace. I think that a confirmation . . .'

121

'Of course,' Scalambri said, 'of course.' And with a generosity as unusual for him as it was unexpected to me: 'Come along too.'

By lift to the eighth floor, then by a short flight of stairs boxed in by a sort of trapdoor, we climbed out on to the wide terrace paved with glazed tiles and into the blinding sunshine.

On the spot by the parapet from whence Voltrano had dropped like a dead weight onto the pile of bricks there were blood stains.

'That clinches it,' said the Inspector, self-satisfied, happy. He even rubbed his hands together. 'And now we must find the object,' peering around, 'with which that son of a bitch struck him.'

'I think,' I ventured, 'that the object with which he struck him, the murderer most likely threw it down. At once, after striking. As soon as he saw Voltrano crumple up.'

'He might have put it down in case Voltrano rallied — so as to have it handy,' the Inspector objected.

'Perhaps. But whether he threw the object first and then Voltrano or Voltrano first and then the object . . .'

'You mean that in either case the object would have been thrown down . . . Yes. He wouldn't have taken it to his room.' And he added: 'I'll go down and look for it.'

'You'd better look for it a bit further than where Voltrano fell,' I called after him, fully self-confident by now.

We remained, Scalambri and I, on the terrace where the sun, but for a gentle breeze, would have been intolerable. The policeman on guard by the stairs, some distance away, was apparently asleep on his feet like a mule. And as we stared down waiting to see the Inspector emerge, Scalambri said, confident and condescending: 'You see, the manner in which the second crime was committed, the brick or stone with which Voltrano was struck are of little or no concern to me. What interests me is why Voltrano was killed. And I know that. Voltrano was killed because he knew who Michelozzi's murderer was and wanted to blackmail him.'

'But you knew that ever since it became clear that the meeting between the murderer and his second victim took place here on the terrace. Had Voltrano been attacked in his room, thrown from the window of his room, you wouldn't have been so sure.'

'Agreed, agreed. I wouldn't have been so sure. But the suspicion that Voltrano knew something more than he said and that he wanted to make use of it to blackmail the murderer, that I'd got since this morning.'

'Whereas I, this morning, believed he was telling the truth, that he didn't know any more than he said he did, that he really couldn't remember . . .'

'You thought he was sincere, upset and almost apologetic at not being able recall with greater precision, at not remembering better . . . But that man never told the truth in his life, not even about what he'd had for breakfast, not even about the time he'd caught his train. On principle. And if he said what he said deceiving you (but not me) as he knew how to deceive, he undoubtedly had some purpose. And do you know what I believe? Most probably he'd seen nothing. He'd made up that impression, he was pretending he'd that vague memory — because of a reckoning he'd made during the reconstruction we were carrying out . . . A minute ago I told you that this morning I'd suspected Voltrano might know . . . I was wrong. Voltrano knew nothing. But as soon as he realized that, being on Michelozzi's left he might have seen something, he reckoned that if he said he'd had the impression someone had perhaps crept up between himself and Michelozzi, that person would do all he could to block his memory — all he could, that is, by paying for his silence in favours or in cash, as is the custom in those circles . . . But he hadn't reckoned with the fact that a man who has already committed one murder may well, if the need arises, commit a second . . .'

'You knew him well it seems.'

'Very well. I knew him very well. He gave me more trouble than all the rest put together. Cunning, treacherous. And ruthless in his most treacherous schemes . . . A fox — and he came up against a wolf.'

'So according to you this morning, when he said what he said, Voltrano was casting his bait blindly without knowing

123

who would rise to it.'

'I'm almost certain of it.'

'Whereas this morning you thought he already knew who was going to bite . . . But whether he knew or not you could have had him watched, unobtrusively shadowed . . .'

'That idiot of an Inspector. I told him Voltrano hadn't convinced me . . . However, this second crime can only fortuitously, by accident lead us to the murderer. The real problem, the one where the clues that will solve the two must be sought, is the first. The motive for the second was clearly blackmail. But it's not a motive that leads to the criminal. If, on the other hand, we can find the motive for the first we've got the criminal cornered . . . But the fact is that of motives among this lot you can find thousands. So many and so various, in fact, it's a miracle they don't gore and butcher each other before our very eyes.'

'An insoluble problem then.'

'Not necessarily . . . You see, Michelozzi was a peculiar man, different from the rest. He was a thief all right. Someone who in the old days I'd have booked a hundred times over for private and public embezzlement, corruption, all the offences tabulated and foreseen by legislators in the administration of public money. But according to current ethics, to the practices of this day and age, he was rigorously honest — and simply because he stole very little, perhaps nothing at all, for himself. All these gentlemen own houses, villas, model farms. They have shares in small, medium and big industries. For years they've been sending money to Switzerland, thousands, millions . . . Not Michelozzi. He hadn't a house or a plot of land to his name. He lodged with nuns and priests. It's even said that he gave part of his salary to the poor . . . Though where he managed to find any poor I don't know . . . His peculiarity in fact consisted in this: not one of this bunch was in a position to blackmail him by threatening to disclose some embezzlement or corruption, for the simple reason that they had all, and I repeat all, profited by Michelozzi's offences. A man who's been corrupted can't bring about his corruptor's downfall without being dragged under himself . . .'

'Impossible then to blackmail him . . .'

'But possible to put pressure on him by other means — to obtain the intervention of higher powers, of Don Gaetano for instance. Don Gaetano manipulates and moulds the consciences of all these chaps like wax. And if Don Gaetano had told Michelozzi to do or not do something in favour of the man who was forced to commit murder instead . . . But there! I've just said it: instead. Instead of resorting to Don Gaetano . . . And is it possible that, before embarking on such extreme, such desperate, such risky measures the murderer didn't play that last card, resort to Don Gaetano? Ah; Here at last is something solid: Don Gaetano knows everything. I've got that far.'

'And there you'll stay.'

'Yes, yes. I know. But I'll have to try.'

From below whence our attention had wandered, the Inspector was shouting his triumph — he'd found and was brandishing on high the *corpus delicti*: a reddish object ensconced in the pristine whiteness of a napkin.

Scalambri tried. For a good three hours. He emerged exhausted, defeated. From what he told me, Don Gaetano had eluded and frustrated each of his questions, exuding Christian doctrine. 'Like a gas,' Scalambri said. 'As if he'd turned on the gas and I'd sat there waiting to be overcome by the fumes . . . The hypocrite, the scoundrel . . .' But wearily he hadn't the energy even to be angry. However he rallied when the Inspector, shortly before going down to the refectory, told him that until the moment Michelozzi was murdered, there'd been five women at the hotel — and that they'd disappeared.

'And you've waited until now to tell me?'

'I've only just found out and I'm telling you . . .'

'Earlier. You should have known earlier. At once. As soon as it happened.' Scalambri retorted.

The Inspector raised his arms slightly, his head inclined towards his left shoulder — a crucifixion.

'It's not important,' I said coming to his rescue. 'I'm quite sure they've nothing to do with the crime. And if they vanished, if they were spirited away that very night without anyone being any the wiser we can only suppose it's because Don Gaetano wanted to avoid an unnecessary scandal.'

'Precisely,' Scalambri chuckled, malevolent, vindictive. 'Precisely . . .' It was clear that he was going to make use of this incident to persuade Don Gaetano to tell him something about the crime — or simply to have his revenge. And he was unable to resist the temptation to mention it at lunch — a blunder, since once Don Gaetano had realized that Scalambri knew about the women and threatened to create a scandal he was on his guard and ready to counterattack.

As though out of idle curiosity Scalambri asked: 'Tell me, is this a hotel or, how should I say, a sort of monastery, or retreat?'

'It's a hotel which periodically becomes, as you say, a sort of monastery.'

'But I mean, it's run like a hotel, isn't it?'

'What do you mean, run like a hotel?' Don Gaetano was already on the alert, wary.

'I mean does it have to conform to the same legal standards, the same police regulations as hotels that are run by non-ecclesiastical or religious organizations?'

'I don't know,' said Don Gaetano.

'But surely someone must.'

'Certainly.' He tinkled the little bell that was in front of his place and in the silence which followed he called: 'Father Cilestri . . .'

From his table the bearer of that name got up. 'Stay, stay where you are,' Don Gaetano said. 'Just tell the Chief Inspector, who would like to know, whether we are obliged to register our guests and to send copies of our registers to the police.' And lowering his voice and turning to Scalambri: 'I presume that is, in fact, what you want to know.'

'We are required to do so,' said Father Cilestri.

'Thank you,' said Don Gaetano. Then to Scalambri: 'So. We are required to do so. But I very much doubt that Father Cilestri has ever done it.'

'Why?'

'How why?' the Minister intervened. 'Because here, my dear Prosecutor, we are among friends — as in a sort of monastery, to use your precise words.'

'A sort of monastery. But it isn't a monastery.'

'Not in theory, but in practice. We are gathered here every year, in three or four sessions, to meditate, to pray . . .' The Minister had obviously forgotten the two crimes. And who would have been tactless enough to remind him?

The Inspector was. When he saw that nobody, either from fear or surprise, was prepared to take the plunge: 'Two crimes, Minister, two.' He told me later; 'What do I care? I'm retiring in a couple of months.'

The Minister turned crimson with rage but restrained himself. 'You, Inspector, are welcome to your opinions. But you have nothing, not a single proof, not a single clue with which to contest my own. And I believe that none of those present in this hall has committed the two crimes.'

'You say none of those present,' Scalambri interjected.

'Exactly. None of those present.'

'Of those present,' Scalambri echoed meaningfully.

'Of those present,' the Minister replied. But with just a hint of hesitation, as though suspecting a trap. Then worried turning to Don Gaetano: 'Is someone missing?'

'No one,' said Don Gaetano with exasperated firmness. And he fixed on Scalambri a gaze which gradually contracted like a camera lense and, losing its apparent lifelessness became quick and piercing. And this alteration in his gaze was accompanied by a gesture of his hand like a cat protracting and retracting its claws.

'Then if no one is missing,' the Minister proceeded, 'I maintain and adhere to my opinion: the murderer is not among us.'

Since he had raised his voice and since from the moment Don Gaetano had spoken to Father Cilestri all were silently following the conversation at our table, the Minister's words were greeted with a chorus of: 'Very true! Quite right! Bravo!' and then with prolonged applause.

When these had subsided the Minister said: 'I'm glad to see

127

that you all share my opinion,' rising in his chair and turning ninety degrees to the right and ninety degrees to the left.

'Had you expected anyone to think otherwise?' Don Gaetano asked mockingly. It was as though he'd thrown a glass of cold water in the Minister's face. It cut his breath. He gasped for words. But said nothing.

Don Gaetano on the other hand had immediately gone on talking. But changing the subject, that is reverting to what he and Scalambri had been discussing earlier. 'Yes, I'm afraid Father Cilestri has always neglected to transmit the files to the police. Is it a serious infringement?'

'For an ordinary hotel manager, yes, very serious.'

'You mean that I'm not an ordinary hotel manager. Thank you.'

'His Excellency intimated as much,' Scalambri said with a glance at the Minister.

'But I said it like that, as a private opinion. Without thinking, without knowing. And especially without the least intention of meddling, of interfering . . . Besides I'm not Minister of the Interior or of Justice. I've other things to think about, thank goodness.'

'He had no intention of granting us a privilege,' Don Gaetano added. 'But allow me — leaving aside for the moment the very serious infringement we (or rather I) inadvertently committed — to tell you in all due conviviality and, I trust you'll believe me, in the friendliest spirit, what I thought when you asked that first question *ex abrupto* (and I naturally use the expression with artful reference to the procedure to which it once gave its name . . . once? a conventional and undeserved compliment to our age, since every procedure we call legal occurred and still occurs *ex abrupto* even if time and custom have made this less obvious). So, when you first asked the question, whether this was a hotel or a sort of monastery — and I believe it would have been more apt to ask whether it was a hotel or a house of fellowship — I immediately thought . . .'
He paused waiting for a sign from Scalambri, some gesture of encouragement.

'Go on,' Scalambri said. Not without a certain anxiety.

128

'I thought: so here we are at table breaking the same bread, drinking the same wine. But he doesn't forget that he's an Inquisitor and a Judge, just as I don't forget that I am a Priest . . . What terrible missions ours are! Terrible and necessary, and necessary insofar as they are terrible . . . Good Lord!' He took his head in his hands, elbows resting on the table and covering his eyes as though in an effort to contemplate within himself all that terrible necessity.

He made a considerable impression. Even on me, I must admit. Only the Inspector went on looking at him and at us with unrestrained irony.

When Don Gaetano surfaced from his inner contemplation, letting his hands drop palms upwards as though to expose the stigmata of the crucifixion from which he had descended, he said: 'But if being a Priest terrifies me how much more would it terrify me to be a Judge . . . Christ's words are marvellous: "Judge not that ye be not judged." He doesn't proscribe judging, but sets it in direct and inevitable relation to being judged. ". . . first cast out the beam out of thine own eye; and then shalt thou see clearly to cast out the mote out of thy brother's eye." You see? The beam in the eye of the one who judges, the mote in the eye of the one who's judged. Can he have wished to imply that only the most sinful people judge, choose to judge, are able to judge by virtue of their sins, of their sin, but after having confessed it and been absolved?' Scalambri was painfully, intensely attentive. And to give him a break — like a cat with a mouse — Don Gaetano digressed: 'The beam . . . Ever since the first time I read that passage, or heard it, I've always thought of Polyphemus blinded by Ulysses, Polyphemus pulling the burning beam out of his eye . . . And who knows if Jesus may not have heard perhaps the tale of Ulysses from some bard, some itinerant salesman . . . Think of how little we know about Jesus's life — as if each of us were to find proof of his own existence from the time when I, say, was ordained priest, you came to the Bench, the Inspector joined the police force, the Professor' [meaning myself] 'had his first exhibition and so on . . . So that our lives would only count insofar as I'm a Priest, you a Judge, the Inspector an Inspector and the Professor a Painter. But childhood, adolescence, youth? And all the books we've read, the love affairs, the betrayals? And we could even forget about adolescence, youth . . . since a man is what the first ten years of his life have made him: we know nothing about him if we know nothing of those ten years. Of course Jesus's life has nothing to do with ours. It's enough to know the years which shone forth, the years which were witnessed. But I've always been fascinated by his years of obscurity, they've always appealed to my imagination.' Then to Scalambri: 'What sort of a childhood did you have? Happy? Unhappy? I hope for your sake it was unhappy. A happy childhood is conducive to boredom, depression, iniquity . . .' And suddenly pulling himself together, repentant: 'Don't take that as a question. Don't answer. It's a weakness I have. When I begin to take an interest in someone I can't help wondering about his childhood . . . But here it's you who ask the questions, not me. So . . . What was I saying?' He paused as if to enable us, his prompters, to give him his cue. But he was quite capable of finding it for himself. And indeed: 'I was talking about judging, about investigating and judging. And about Christ wanting perhaps to make it clear that only the worst sinners can undertake such a task — only the last can be first in these circumstances. But for pity's sake don't see in my ramblings the slightest personal allusion. I know nothing about you. Nothing, absolutely.' And in saying this he fixed Scalambri with a gaze that seemed to imply that, on the contrary, he knew everything . . . 'And on the other hand the words "worst" and "best", I use them in the evangelical sense — precisely of the first who will be the last, the last who will be the first,' His face lit up with benevolence, with affection. 'I know nothing about you,' again he lingered on 'nothing', turning it into 'everything', 'but I love you.'

When Scalambri got up he seemed a different man. He leant on my arm heavily, almost unsteady. And when the Inspector came to ask him in an undertone: 'Do we go into this matter of the vanishing women, sir?' he snapped rather louder than was required and so as to be heard by all those who unobtrusively

130

clustered around us: 'What's the use of going into it? Don't you understand that those women, if they were here at all, have nothing to do with the murders and that if we go chasing after them we risk losing the thread altogether?'

'Which thread?' the Inspector asked innocently. He was enjoying himself.

'The thread . . .' Scalambri said vaguely, lowering his voice. 'The thread . . . money, profits, their private concerns, blackmail. The only one we have.'

'Except that we haven't got it . . .' said the Inspector.

'We haven't got it, all right . . .' Scalambri's voice shook hysterically. 'All right we haven't got it. But we must try to get hold of it, to grasp it . . . I've already taken measures. Colleagues of mine in various places are making enquiries. I'm not idle for my part . . .' He dragged me away leaving the Inspector standing. I glanced back at him. He was satisfied, the Inspector, satisfied and grinning. And he winked at me as much as to say: 'He's in a bad way, your friend.' And indeed Scalambri was saying to me: 'That fool of an Inspector! He wants to chase after those women when we don't even know if they really existed.'

'They did.'

'Oh? They really did . . . However that's neither here nor there . . . You see I've got a very clear opinion of these two crimes which I think I mentioned to you earlier when we were up on the terrace. Therefore I want to get rid of all the dross, all the details and clues which would only put us on the wrong track, confuse the issue . . . The Inspector, either in good faith because he's a fool or for reasons of his own, because he's an untrustworthy fool, plants these women in my path as a stumbling block to trip me up. But I'll step over it and carry on regardless.'

I charitably refrained from reminding him that shortly before going to the refectory it was he, not the Inspector, who'd found the presence of the women, and their subsequent disappearance, significant.

'Don Gaetano seems anxious to keep the presence of these women from becoming public knowledge. And insofar as he's anxious . . . Think of what the papers would make of it if it emerged that the spiritual exercises of five of those prominent men were relieved by the presence of their mistresses . . .'

'Apart from the fact that not a single paper, I repeat not a single one would mention it . . . What do you think would happen? A few people might be shocked, most would be amused and one or two of the women would be approached with a view toward making a film — a film called something like *Spiritual Exercises*, with the woman naked and surrounded by a crowd of lewd men . . . But what would happen to me would be first that my boss would take over the inquest; second he would promote me; and third he'd transfer me. And the two crimes would be filed away as "committed by persons unknown". Do you think that's worth it?'

'So you're determined to solve them, to find the criminal?'

'I hope so, I hope so . . .' But without conviction. Then suddenly curious, spiteful: 'And what do they look like, these women? Young? Beautiful? And who did they belong to?'

'Not bad–looking, youngish. The type that appeals to such men: on the plump side, rather showy, rather common. There's a clear distinction for these chaps between women one marries, with whom one begets children, and women with whom one commits adultery. The latter must exhale sin at first sight, at first smell . . . But to whom they belonged, the five who were here, I don't know.'

'I'll have to know. That at least I'll have to know.'

'It could come in handy,' I said ambiguously.

'It won't be of any use but I must know. Either Don Gaetano tells me or I'll summon these gentlemen one by one.'

'I think that if you promise to hold your tongue Don Gaetano will tell you.'

'I think so too,' Scalambri said. He patted me patronizingly on the back and went away. Presumably in search of Don Gaetano.

Finding me on my own the Minister came up. I received a second patronizing pat on the back. 'My dear friend,' he greeted me, shaking his head, distressed, disconsolate, that we should be there, mixed up in worldly affairs, crime, hobnobbing

132

with judges, with the police, men like him and me who had
nothing to do with such things, who were equally though
diversely innocent — since according to him the innocent
pointlessness of art conferred on the artist an innocence comparable to that which his Christian life-style conferred on him,
albeit without, needless to say, the distinction and loftiness of
his Christian life-style.

I expressed what he intimated: 'A terrible experience. I'd
never have suspected, when I drove up that lane to the Hermitage, that I'd be involved in this nightmare!'

'And what about me? I come here year after year as to a place
of renewal, of enlightenment. Could I have foreseen anything
of the sort . . . ? Two crimes, two of my dearest, closest
friends killed in a matter of hours. And every one of us tarnished
with the suspicions of the Prosecutor, the press, the public . . .
Not simply tarnished. Actually infected by suspicion. Did you
hear the Inspector at lunch? Duty, professional concern, that's
all very well. But good God, a little consideration, a little tact
. . . And not on account of who we are, what each of us stands
for in public life — no question of that, the law is equal for all
. . . But because of the place, the reason for which we're here:
meditation, prayer . . .' And having come to the point he'd
been leading up to: 'I hope your friend the Prosecutor doesn't
see things in the same perspective as the Inspector. For it's all a
matter of perspective, of intellectual perspective, of moral
perspective.'

'He's a sphinx.'

'What?'

'My friend, the Prosecutor. He's a sphinx. He doesn't give
anything away as regards his views on the crimes, his plans
. . . When I ask him what he thinks he answers in riddles.'

'They're all alike, these public prosecutors. Oracles, that's
what they are, oracles . . . But mind you, they don't play the
oracle because they know and don't want to say. They play the
oracle just as from time immemorial the role of oracle has
always been played.'

'And yet, you know, Scalambri may have discovered something, may have got hold of some clue.'

133

'Do you think so?' the Minister said trying hard to appear ironically incredulous.

'Yes. It seems to me that he's got hold of something — some indication, some information.'

'Some indication, some information,' the Minister echoed, his mask of ironic incredulity suddenly dropping. 'And what could it possibly be, this indication, this information?'

'Not having known the victims, not knowing anything about their characters, their interests, their concerns, I'm not in a position to decipher Scalambri's riddles.'

'For instance . . .' In the hope that I might recall something.

'For instance just now, referring to the crimes, he said: "Nobody deserves to be praised for his virtue if he's not capable of being wicked."'

'"Nobody deserves to be praised for his virtue if he's not capable of being wicked" . . . Is that what he said?'

'Just that,' I said silently completing the quotation: '"All other virtue is generally no more than laziness or lack of determination".'

'It sounds like one of those proverbs one used to find in chocolate wrappers . . . "Nobody deserves to be praised for his virtue if he's not capable of being wicked . . ." And as proverbs go I'd say it was most inept. Whoever is capable of being wicked is wicked.' And having put François de la Rochefoucauld in his place, the Minister was racking his brains to find out what significance this inept proverb might have in relation to the present circumstances. 'Maybe he was referring to poor Michelozzi. He was naturally virtuous . . . But what has that to do with it? He wasn't murdered on account of his virtue . . . Since everybody said he was virtuous — and I say so myself who was close to him for almost half a century — the man who killed him wanted to put an end to the threat Michelozzi represented for him. There's no other explanation.'

'So you don't believe it was an accident any more?'

'An accident? How could I believe such a thing after the second murder?'

'But if you maintain that the murderer wasn't one of you . . .'

'We aren't the only people here. I believe there must be

between twenty and thirty people who come in and go out of this hotel. And they're the least obtrusive, those who, because they're where they have to be and do what they have to do, are practically invisible.'

I thought of the cook's anxiety and how justified it was. 'But a waiter, a scullery maid, one of those Ursulines or Daughters of Mary who help serve at table, what reason would they have to kill Michelozzi and then Voltrano?'

'Have you never heard of hired murderers, of professional killers? Things, my dear friend, are usually less complicated than they seem to be or than we make them.' He patted me on the back — pityingly this time. And he went to join a group of acquaintances, probably to report La Rochefoucauld's maxim which I'd fancifully attributed to Scalambri.

I entered the hotel just as Scalambri was emerging from Don Gaetano's study. He was happy, relishing in his heart of hearts the secret Don Gaetano had doubtless imparted to him. So blissfully happy he passed close by without noticing me. I went towards Don Gaetano's study, knocked, opened the door.

Don Gaetano was at his desk. He raised his eyes from his papers saying: 'Come in.' His eyes and his glasses. Since when his eyes were raised his glasses, perched mid-way down his nose, were no longer aligned with his gaze but possessed a gaze of their own, less cold and impassive. A disturbing illusion caused by the refraction of the tinted lampshade at his side — a glass shade, one of those which at the beginning of the century were made in Nancy and Vienna but are now shoddily reproduced almost everywhere. It was speckled green, yellow, blue and predominantly purple and the light it cast on the glasses was mobile, so that it seemed to animate them while Don Gaetano's eyes remained dead.

Whoever reads this manuscript or, if it's ever published, this book, may wonder why I've said nothing more till now about Don Gaetano's glasses. Well, I haven't said anything more because it's not true that they had made little impression the first time I saw him take them out; but maybe they impressed me less at the time than when I thought about them and saw

135

them later. Undoubtedly in fact, since I began to realize how uneasy those glasses made me when, in my room I found myself sketching them. Over and over again on a single sheet of paper. So that a crop of spectacles emerged like a crop of melons — large, small, barely outlined, without lenses, with lenses. And some with Don Gaetano's unseeing eyes behind them. Nothing like the sketches I usually make — and someone seeing this one without having read these lines might imagine I'd been immersed in Spinoza who made lenses of this kind. Or that I'd been impressed by the glasses of Don Antonio de Solis in that portrait which adorns the title-page of the eighteenth-century edition of his *Istoria della conquista del Messico*. Or that I was trying to illustrate the poems of that Arab-Sicilian poet on lenses. And now as I write, the fact that I recall these images (actual images or word images) amazes me and increases my anxiety. Why should I see Spinoza in his optician's workshop so clearly — the shades of evening, the lenses like tiny lakes in an illuminated manuscript within the forests of written words (that cramped seventeenth-century script which seems to be buffeted by the wind)? That I recall so vividly the portrait of Don Antonio, the verses of Ibn Hamdis? Can there be something about lenses, glasses, which arouses in me a remote, undefinable sense of wonder and, simultaneously of apprehension? Can it be something to do with the truth and the fear of discovering it? (And there came to my mind a tale by Anna Maria Ortese called *Un Paio di occhiali* about a very short-sighted little girl who is finally given a pair of spectacles — and the squalor of the Neapolitan alley where she lives, now suddenly revealed to her, makes her giddy and sick).

But to return to Don Gaetano's glasses, to the anxiety they provoked — was it by chance that they were an exact replica of those worn by the devil or had he acquired them on purpose? More than once I'd been tempted to ask him. But I'd always refrained.

'I hope I'm not disturbing you,' I said.

'Nobody ever disturbs me.' And after scrutinizing me at length, but as usual as though he didn't see me: 'Is something troubling you? Or are you planning to leave us?'

136

'I don't think it would be possible for me to leave. Besides I'm curious to see how it's all going to end.'

'It won't end. Your curiosity will not be satisfied . . . Is something troubling you? I mean is there something you'd like to know, something you'd like to tell me? At the moment everybody here wants either to know something or to impart something to me.'

'Yes there's something I'd like to ask you.'

'Good. Ask away.' And he raised his glasses to the level of his eyes. Not to see me better. That was obvious.

'This evening at dinner, I don't know at what precise moment you shot your arrow but I saw it, quivering still, stuck in Scalambri's side.'

'A nice image. Very literary.' He smiled enigmatically, perhaps with pleasure. 'The arrow, the side — indeed a nice image . . . and still quivering. I can even admit to having seen it myself. But I didn't shoot it.'

'Do you mean you shot so many that you don't know which one reached the target?'

He didn't answer.

'Poor Scalambri,' I said after a while, not knowing how to re-connect with Don Gaetano who was waiting for me to speak or to go.

'Poor. There you have a word which is always being mis-used.'

'I don't think I've misused it, from a Christian point of view. I saw him then naked and bleeding, therefore at that moment poor. To clothe the naked, to visit the infirm . . . Or does my memory mislead me?'

'From a Christian point of view . . . So you have a Christian point of view.'

'I'm playing the Devil's advocate.'

'An interesting part. I played it once in earnest. At a Canonization. Amusing too . . . However your memory does not mislead you — to clothe the naked, to visit the infirm . . . But five minutes ago Scalambri was sitting where you are now, fully clothed and in excellent health . . . He was blackmailing me.'

137

'You don't say so!' I said in feigned surprise.

'Don't pretend you didn't know or, if you didn't know that you don't understand.'

'You're right. But was it altogether blackmail?'

'Not altogether. But while assuring me of his silence about the women he wanted me to break mine — out of courtesy in exchange for his courtesy, if not out of gratitude.'

'And you?'

'I was grateful.'

'More than courteous then.'

'Those five names, he could have got them from anybody here. And I gave him five stories to go with them. Your friend really enjoyed them. He was like a dog who has at last been thrown a bone to gnaw — he growled with satisfaction, with pleasure.'

'He's not my friend. If he were I wouldn't be able to share your scorn.'

'Ah, so you despise him? I don't. It isn't scorn I feel. I feel nothing for your friend — I'm sorry, for the Prosecutor — just as I feel nothing for the odd cog or spring in that clock,' pointing to the clock on his desk.

'But you do for the clock.'

'I wouldn't say so. Unless you call feelings my annoyance when I want to know the time and it's stopped.'

'Just the contrary of what you'd feel for Scalambri if, looking at him to make sure he's stopped you found he was advancing — advancing, that is, towards the culprit.'

'You're going to repeat what you said yesterday — that I ought to help Scalambri solve the problem. But the problem is Scalambri's not mine.'

'Professionally it's Scalambri's, only professionally. If we were here in complete isolation, outside every jurisdiction, don't you think we'd be obliged to invent for ourselves the law Scalambri represents and to look for the culprit?'

'The contrary is equally possible — that we'd all become guilty, each one of us towards the others. And in fact what you call inventing the law is nothing else — all becoming guilty. But let's forget it. We don't know where we'd end up . . .

138

We're not isolated, we're not outside every jurisdiction. Your friend Scalambri is here. He has all the authority and all the means to solve the problem . . . And this time I won't apologize for calling him your friend . . . Whether you despise him or not, you're on his side, you can only be on his side.'

'Yes I can only be on his side. You, on the other hand . . .'

'I have no side to be on. I'm waiting for everything to be accomplished.'

'That is, for everything not to be accomplished.'

'From your point of view, yes — for everything not to be accomplished. But from mine . . . Do you remember St Luke's Gospel? Have you ever read it? . . . "I have come to send fire on the earth; and what will I, if it be already kindled? But I have a baptism to be baptised with, and how am I straitened till it be accomplished!"'

'What baptism are you waiting for?'

'Suffering, death — there is no other.'

'But to wait for such a baptism, what need have you for all this? Why did you have to build a hotel, to manage it, to do and manage so many things? What need have your friends to rule, to command — with your blessing if not indeed as your agents?'

'It's now my turn to protest — they are not my friends. But they too are the fire that's kindled. And insofar as I despise them at the same time as I love them: "What will I, if it is already kindled?"'

'So all must be consumed.'

'There's no other way. There's no other issue. To consume, to consume . . . Our greatest mistake, the greatest mistake which has been committed by those who governed, or who thought they governed, Christ's Church has been to identify with a type of society, with a type of order. It's a mistake which persists even though there are many who now begin to realize that it's a mistake. To put it more or less in a nutshell: the eighteenth century made us lose our senses, the twentieth will make us recover them again. But what am I saying, will make us recover them again? It will be the final victory, our triumph.'

'The end.'

'From your point of view, yes, the end . . . But it will be the most Christian, or at least the beginning of the most Christian era the world can achieve . . . Everything concurs, everything is on our side. Even the things which those of us who lost their senses or have not yet recovered them believed and believe to be against us . . . Science is on our side, surfeit is on our side. And so too, of course, are ignorance and famine on our side . . . Think of it: science . . . We opposed it so violently! And in the end when it examines the cells, the atoms, the stars in the heavens, when it extracts some secret, when it splits, when it explodes, when it sends men off for a walk on the moon — what is it doing if not increasing the terror Pascal experienced before the universe?'

'The men of today don't seem to me to be overwhelmed by such terror. Quite the reverse.'

'They're too busy redefining frontiers, as if after a successful war, to experience it. But the cracks through which that terror will seep are there already. And the cosmic terror will be as nothing compared to man's terror of himself and of others . . . Remember? "And I shall always oppose him till he understands that he is an incomprehensible monster"; and since today as never before God opposes us . . .'

'. . . we flee from God.'

'There is no flight from God. It's not possible. The flight from God is a march towards God.' He said it with a certain hopelessness. Or so it seemed to me. For removing at that moment his glasses and closing as though in weariness his eyes, his face appeared suddenly fragile and aloof, as of someone who has grown old in captivity and remembers that once he had attempted to escape.

With his eyes still closed (either because he could read my thoughts or because it was I who'd read his) he said: 'Escape . . .' He opened his eyes, leant towards me across the desk: 'It's been said that Voltaire's rationalism has a theological basis which is no less incommensurate with man than Pascal's. For my part I'd go so far as to say that Candide's candour is worth precisely as much as Pascal's terror — or indeed that it's the same thing. Except that Candide finally found a garden of his own to cultivate . . . "Il faut cultiver son jardin . . ." Impossible. There's been a general and final expropriation. Maybe today one should rewrite all the books that have ever been written. And in fact we do nothing else, opening them with skeleton keys . . . All of them except *Candide*.'

'But we can read it.'

He shrugged. 'Read it.' Then briskly: 'Indeed, you must read it. So as to convince yourself that you're alone and there is no help.' Then kindly: 'But why do you want to repress all that leads you to us? Why do you oppose yourself?'

'Because you oppose me. Because your God opposes me. I'm not an incomprehensible monster.'

I got up. For once I would be the one to leave.

'Good night,' I said. He didn't answer.

I wasted no time going to my room after leaving Don Gaetano's study — the time it took to cross the corridor and the hall, summon the lift, go up, walk along nearly two sides of the quadrangle the corridors formed on each landing, open my door, switch on the light, go in. I describe my movements as I recall them, and I believe I recall them correctly. But on second thoughts I may have waited longer for the lift than I believe. Otherwise how am I to account for the fact that on my table, conspicuous against the sheets of white drawing paper, was a black-bound volume — one of those bindings the French call Janseniste. It bore no title either on the front or the spine, but I knew before opening it that it was Pascal's *Pensées*. How Don Gaetano had been able to have it conveyed to my room before I got there can only be explained by that loss of time, as I said, unperceived by myself. Unless he'd had it conveyed earlier. A much more disturbing explanation.

I opened it at the title page and then at the place where a black ribbon book-mark had been set. My eye naturally fell on the right hand page which began with number 426 (the number of the *pensée*, not the page) — and my mind wandered off on a fantasy of numbered thoughts, that all the thoughts of

141

each and all of us, whether written, spoken or simply thought, were nothing but numberings and numbers swallowed, absorbed and calculated by an immense, invisible machine. I read it, *pensée* 426: 'La vraie nature étant perdue, tout devient sa nature; comme, le véritable bien étant perdu, tout devient son véritable bien.' And then the others up to number 443.

Had the book-mark been placed there by chance or had Don Gaetano set it there for me?

I preferred not to think about it nor to continue reading. I closed the book and put it aside. And I began to sketch. Since it was the sketch I'd promised Scalambri I drew a female nude, as obscene and unpleasant as I was able. So that Scalambri, if I knew him as well as I thought I did, would get rid of it by selling it — and according to the price it would fetch, precisely by so much would he appreciate and envy me.

For me drawing, once I've chosen my theme or subject, is such an automatic process that my hand, and my eyes, seem to become detached, independent, moving on their own and somehow delivering me from a weight, a dross. By thinking of anything but the drawing when I draw my mind becomes more precise, alert, consistent. And my memory grows more distinct and active. And so, sketching this nude for Scalambri, I worked out a theory I'd happened to formulate after the first murder. I worked it out, that is, as Charles Auguste Dupin works out his theories in Poe's tales. While my hand and eyes wandered over the sheet of paper my mind wandered over the space in front of the hotel — a semi-circle of about a hundred metres in depth in the direction of the wood. I perceived every stone, every dent, every tree — as if I'd been looking out of the window of my room in full daylight. But I shall say no more. I finished the sketch when I felt I'd solved the problem. Very laboured, overdrawn and doodled over, the sketch. But the solution to the problem was distinct and almost obvious — very similar to the solution of Poe's *Purloined Letter*. And putting off its verification till the next morning I went to bed and fell asleep at once.

The first person I saw next morning was the Inspector. He was in the hall sitting in an armchair reading through the papers. With meaningful irony he immediately announced: 'We've found the thread.'

'And what is it, this thread?'

'The one the Prosecutor was after. But what am I saying the thread? Hundreds of threads. All very tangled . . . A pile this high,' measuring the height from the ground to his knee, 'of photocopies of cheques. All signed by Michelozzi on the private or secret funds of which he disposed . . . The Prosecutor'll go mad.' And he contemplated blissfully the picture he'd evoked of Scalambri going mad.

'But are these cheques made out to one of those present?'

'To one? To all of them. There isn't a single one who hasn't his share.'

'What then?'

'Then, from all these cheques hundreds of minor cases of misappropriation may be deduced, of embezzlement. Or one gigantic case. But a murder case never.'

'I agree.'

'The Prosecutor on the other hand is convinced that the key to the first murder, and therefore to the second, he'll find it among those cheques . . . Not that his theory is entirely unsound. But it's so hard to prove it might just as well be . . . His argument is as follows: Michelozzi gave those people money not to go and squander it on women or deposit it in Switzerland. He gave it to them for the Party, for factions within the Party, groups, patronage, private patrons. One of them would instead have kept it for himself — all of it, not just a greater or lesser percentage as is the custom. Michelozzi, suspecting or discovering this would have threatened . . .'

'Threatened what? He couldn't denounce the culprit . . .'

'Threatened not to give him any more . . .'

'But he'd have found it elsewhere.'

'That's what I say . . . However there may be something positive in the Prosecutor's theory — if we twist it another way . . . I'd say what if Michelozzi had realized that some money he was giving someone had been used to finance debauchery, iniquity? Or what if he'd even been aware of this all the time but now wanted to withdraw from it, extricate himself from an enterprise he considered too risky?'

'The theory's more convincing put that way. But to take your first hypothesis first, what about Michelozzi's reputation for loving his neighbour as he loved himself?'

'I hope you won't mind my saying so but you just don't know what these home-loving church-going chaps are capable of — men with their noses buried in their prayerbooks, men who boast of loving their neighbour as they love themselves . . . In two months (I can hardly wait) I'll have been thirty years in the police force. Well, the most dastardly crimes that have come my way, the most cold-blooded, the hardest to disentangle as well as the silliest and easiest were committed by men and women whose knees were that swollen,' his hands moulded a great loaf, 'from kneeling at the choir rail and the confessional . . . Some of course were crimes of passion. But most of them, you can take my word for it, were for money. Nearly always for money to be inherited from their nearest and dearest.' He got up. 'I'm going to see what thread he's managed to extract from the tangle, the Public Prosecutor . . . Shall I leave you the papers?'

'No thanks. I'm going for a stroll in the woods.'

And I went. But to check my insight of the previous night.

We all met again in the refectory for lunch. Don Gaetano wasn't exactly merry — he'd probably never been in all his life — but he seemed to be secretly enjoying himself, like someone who has prepared a practical joke and is waiting for the victim, or victims, to fall into the trap. Scalambri was exhausted, red-eyed. And he wasn't all that eager to talk. In the morning I'd sent the sketch to him in his room. He thanked me dryly — obviously he hadn't liked it. The Inspector kept a half-pitying, half-mocking eye on him, glancing at me from time to time with a look that implied: just see how he's worn himself out trying to unravel that endless tangle! The Minister was rather glum — among Michelozzi's cheques, I learnt later, Scalambri had found one made out to him and he'd questioned him.

144

More sombre still was our other table companion, the Director of the bank on which Michelozzi's cheques were drawn whom Scalambri had grilled for a couple of hours — with no other result than the unmitigated hatred which now smouldered in the Director's eyes when they happened to light on the Public Prosecutor.

Scalambri's acknowledgement of the sketch hadn't escaped Don Gaetano's notice: 'What does it represent,' he asked him, 'the picture he gave you?'

'A nude. A female nude.'

'Oh?' said Don Gaetano. As much as to say: and what else?

'An ugly nude,' I said in self-defence.

'Oh.' In a tone which implied: that's better.

'But beautifully done,' Scalambri added out of pure courtesy.

'Obviously. Did you expect that at his age, with his experience, with his reputation, the Professor wouldn't draw beautifully? Most excellently, he must draw. Always. Whenever he draws,' said Don Gaetano. And to me: 'For my part, as I believe I already confessed, I've seen very little of your work. And nearly always in reproduction. But from the little I've seen . . . Now I wonder . . . Have you ever painted or drawn anything concerning our faith? A Christ, a Madonna, a Saint or, I don't know, some religious procession, a church . . . ?'

'A Mary Magdalene some years ago.'

'Of course, a Mary Magdalene . . . And how did you depict her?

'I depicted her . . .'

'No. Stop. Let me guess . . . You depicted her as a retired whore — old, shapeless, piteously and ludicrously got up.'

'You've guessed right.' Reluctantly.

'I'm glad. It means that to a certain extent I've understood you.' And as if the candidate (myself) having answered the first question correctly he could now proceed with the examination: 'And wouldn't you be tempted by the idea of painting here, for us, for the chapel, a Christ? Please note that I use the verb to tempt.'

'It doesn't tempt me,' I replied firmly. But seeing that Don

Gaetano was well pleased with my firmness as with a positive reaction, I changed my tactics. 'After Redon, Rouault . . . No. It doesn't tempt me.'

'You're right,' said Don Gaetano. But well aware, I suspect, that his approval would annoy me. 'After Redon, after Rouault . . . Not to mention earlier names — Grünewald, Giovanni Bellini, Antonello . . . For me one of the most disturbing representations of Christ is the one by Antonello now I believe in the museum of Piacenza — that mask of dull suffering . . . Terrible . . . But in our day, yes, undoubtedly Redon, Rouault . . . Very noble, Rouault's *Miserere* — a Passion which isn't a conclusion but an Annunciation . . . I mean one might almost assume that with Rouault the story of humanity's as it were Christological Passion is concluded, that his is the final expression, the ultimate breath. But instead it begins all over again, is re-enacted . . . But Redon . . . You see, Redon is no less disturbing than Antonello, but differently . . . I refer, of course, to the Christ of the third sequence in his *Tentation* . . . One has the impression — violent, devastating — that it's only through a revelation, a vision, that Redon could have portrayed Christ's face as he has done – that Christ must truly have had such features and that once only, centuries later, he revealed them to Redon . . . Not to the Apostles, not to the Evangelists — for he obviously wanted them to forget his features. To Redon . . . His hands to Saint Teresa of Avila. His features to Redon. Why? . . . I ask you because you certainly know more than me about Redon.'

'I don't know . . . Perhaps because Redon always refused to look at what was naked.'

'What was naked?'

'He used to say: "Je ne regarde jamais ce qui est nu".'

'Because he always went deeper than nakedness. Like x-rays.'

Oddly enough I myself had had, when I saw Redon's Christ, the same impression as Don Gaetano. But I said: 'What you describe derives from a rather trivial fact which has perhaps more to do with vanity than with mystical inspiration — Redon, quite simply, wanted to portray Christ unlike any other.'

'But so unlike, and of such intensity . . . However. You don't want, or you don't feel inclined to have a try at your own interpretation of Christ for us?'

'I don't feel inclined but I want to.'

'Ah, you want to . . . Very good. We shall see.' And as though he'd only at that moment realized that the others were bored, he changed the subject. 'You look tired, Prosecutor.'

'Yes indeed,' sighed the Prosecutor.

'And you look rested Inspector.' With malicious intent.

'Indeed,' Scalambri observed bitterly.

'It's hardly plausible that you should find wearisome what the Inspector takes in his stride. Yet the Inspector . . .'

'The Inspector,' said the Inspector, 'takes his leave in two months. That accounts for his happiness.'

'You're leaving?'

'The Police Force. I'm retiring. To the country.'

'Lucky you!' the Minister exclaimed.

'Because he's leaving the Police Force?' Don Gaetano, smiling ironically, asked the Minister.

'No, no. I wouldn't dream of such a thing. I respect, I admire the Police Force. Because he's retiring to the country.'

'That's an easily acquired bliss — especially in your case, in the Director's . . .' The Director was startled. 'The Inspector has to wait for another two months whereas either of you could do it tomorrow.'

The Minister and the Director looked gloomier than ever. I suppose they suspected Don Gaetano might be referring to the cheques in Scalambri's possession which could, perhaps, make their resignation necessary. And who knows? Don Gaetano may well have been referring precisely to that. They said in chorus: 'I wish it were true!'

'Is it so hard to break away? Do they keep you back by force?' Don Gaetano inquired with feigned innocence and surprise.

'Well . . . Not exactly by force,' the Minister replied. 'But it's certainly not easy to break away.' The Director nodded in agreement.

'Especially just now,' Don Gaetano said ambiguously. Did

he mean that they'd be sacked on the spot or that they'd not leave until they'd accounted for what they'd been up to with Michelozzi? The fact is, he was hinting at something. And he was enjoying himself.

The Minister found the strength to interpret Don Gaetano's words in yet another way: 'Indeed especially now. When things are going badly, to leave would be an evasion, a desertion.'

'A betrayal,' Don Gaetano added ironically.

'And as to going badly, things certainly are going badly,' the Inspector remarked.

'Let's not exaggerate,' said the Minister.

'Let's not exaggerate,' echoed the Director.

'Let's not exaggerate,' concluded Scalambri.

'Well are things going badly or are they not?' Don Gaetano asked all three.

'It depends on the point of view,' the Minister replied.

'From the point of view,' said the Inspector, 'of those who keep their hands in their own pockets things are going very badly.'

There was a silence — as when well-behaved people discover that an ill-bred person is in their midst. Then the Director said: 'It's not a question of keeping one's hands in one's own pockets or in other people's. It's a question . . .'

'. . . of being able to carry on one's tricks and still get something out of one's neighbours' pockets,' I concluded for him. 'Of still being able to find something there.'

'The state isn't a pick-pocket,' the Minister said indignantly.

'Indeed it isn't a pick-pocket,' the Director echoed with more restrained indignation.

'But Gentlemen,' Don Gaetano said to the Minister and the Director, 'I hope you're not going to distress me by saying that the state still exists . . . Considering my age and all the trust I've always had in you it would be an unbearable revelation. I was so sure it didn't exist any more . . .'

The Minister and the Director exchanged a rapid glance and decided to take it as a joke. They laughed. They were still laughing when we left the table.

I was back at the hotel by late afternoon. And I went straight to my room. I'd had an idea for the Christ I'd promised Don Gaetano. Not exactly promised, but in the present circumstances I could consider it as a promise to be kept.

I drew for a couple of hours. My hand was just a fraction tenser than usual. But not a stroke on the page was hesitant or smudged, even imperceptibly. Nothing but this unwonted haste, a sort of rhythm responding as it were to a remote, inner musical tempo. A tempo that refused to become a theme, a phrase which merged and expressed itself in the signs traced on the paper, in the thoughts and images which ran through my head with increasing febrility. And these thoughts and images were not, as usually happens when I draw, of things which have no connection with what I'm drawing and roughly shading (a shading not to be confused with that of the drawing schools — if such things still exist).

Then I heard in the silence of the hotel rising and mounting, spiralling up from the hall, from the first floor through the winding corridors, an excited hubbub, a banging of doors, a scurrying of footsteps. But I didn't move till the sound began to recede again towards the hall and to settle there — a continuous, ever increasing rumble.

The hall was packed as on the day after the first murder. Everybody was questioning everybody else hysterically: 'When? Where? How?'

Don Gaetano had been found dead. But nobody knew whether in his room or in his study or in the chapel or in the wood. Finally someone shouted from outside: 'In the wood by the old mill.' And the herd trooped out on to the esplanade, scattered, re-assembled once again to go funnelling down the narrow path which led to the old mill.

I went with them. The last, bringing up the rear of that somewhat grotesque procession of middle-aged men who practically ran panting and stumbling up the path. I could hear those in front of me asking each other with baited breath if Don Gaetano had been murdered or had died a natural death — as if death, as Don Gaetano should really have taught them, isn't always and everywhere natural.

149

He had been murdered. Near the old mill of which the great millstone was, in fact, a relic. And this millstone from which he had slithered was partly supporting him.

I wasn't unduly impressed seeing him again dead. Death which endows even fools with a certain dignity seemed to have impaired Don Gaetano's. He lay in disarray and as though out of joint. His legs, almost at right angles, stretched his cassock which had been rucked up as he slipped, exposing his thick white woollen socks. And all eyes focused on those socks because they contrasted sharply with the black shoes and the black cassock and because they were winter socks and it was high summer. After the socks one's gaze, or at least mine, was drawn to his glasses which, from the cord attached to his breast, hung down on to a root where they rested at an odd angle to a sunbeam filtering through the foliage — it was like the detail of a painting by a minor pupil of Caravaggio. And I say minor because everything about the dead Don Gaetano and his surroundings was minor — diminished, reduced, low-key in relation to what he'd been alive.

Close by his left hand was a pistol — short and stubby. So close to his hand that one of the onlookers asked if he'd killed himself.

I said: 'Does that seem likely?'

'We all have our fits of depression,' the other replied, vexed. And that he should appear to one of his devotees as similar to all of us confirmed my impression that death, for the time being at any rate and in the present setting, had degraded Don Gaetano.

We stood in a semi-circle some ten paces away from Don Gaetano's body and from Scalambri and the Inspector, who were beside it staring down as if they expected to see it suddenly give signs of life, of awakening.

I went over to Scalambri. With a sneer of satisfied defeat — as if something he'd predicted had come to pass but to his disadvantage, increasing his responsibilities, his duties — he said: '*Omnia bona tria.*' His beloved Latin again! Then suddenly realizing that the phrase might appear to reflect real satisfaction and not the self-pity which had inspired it: 'I mean we're in a pretty mess.' But he'd blundered again with that pretty . . . 'A terrible mess, an incredible mess.' And he resumed his contemplation of the body.

'What worries me . . .' the Inspector muttered as though to himself while he stared at the pistol. He left the sentence in mid-air.

'What worries you?' Scalambri asked, at the very limit of exasperation, implying more or less that what the Inspector thought, his theories, his inferences, his suspicions hindered rather than helped him, Scalambri.

'The pistol,' said the Inspector.

'What about the pistol?' As exasperated as ever.

'About the pistol nothing. About the fact that we've found it — been allowed to find something. Something to worry about.'

'And you find nothing better than to say it *coram populo*?'

'That's why I didn't say it. Only in reply to your question.'

Since there was no adequate reply to this Scalambri took a decisive step — apparently on the spur of the moment but perhaps on the contrary after mature deliberation. Turning to what in his Latin he had called the *populo* he said: 'Please, gentlemen, will you go back to the hotel. And get ready to leave this evening.'

A murmur of protest arose.

'It's a necessary precaution. For your safety, for my responsibility.'

'Quite right,' said the Minister. 'Perhaps it should have been taken earlier.'

Scalambri ignored the reproach. But with greater and fiercer authority he confirmed: 'By this evening the hotel must be vacated. Not a cat must be left behind.'

'A cat,' said Father Cilestri emerging from the crowd and coming up to Scalambri, 'we don't have a cat, we've always used rat poison . . .' Was he trying to deflate Scalambri or was he so upset that he'd taken his words literally? 'But what about me, what about the other priests here with me?'

'Everyone,' Scalambri repeated. 'Everyone. I'm closing the hotel, Father. I'm closing it and affixing the seals.' Then with

greater courtesy: 'Please, gentlemen, go and pack your bags
. . . We have work to do here.'

They left, the Minister in the lead.

As to work, only the photographer was working. Then the
doctor arrived. Then two bearers with a canvas stretcher.
They eased Don Gaetano on to it and carried him off. His
glasses hung down from the stretcher swaying in time to the
bearers' steps.

I followed them to the van drawn up in front of the hotel.
Then I went to my room to get ready to leave.

My suitcases only required locking. I hesitated briefly between
taking or leaving the volume Don Gaetano had sent me the
previous evening. I left it behind — next to the Christ I'd
drawn.

It wasn't yet dark but the hotel was all lit up and seemed,
from the esplanade, and precisely because of all those lights, to
summon the night to come and enfold us. A few cars were
already leaving. Scalambri and the Inspector were supervising
the exodus. I came up to them.

'It didn't take you long,' Scalambri observed with a glance
at my suitcase.

'Understandably enough, you can't wait to be out of this
hell,' said the Inspector.

'If we'd waited much longer,' Scalambri said, 'it would
have ended like that Agatha Christie novel — everyone
murdered one after the other. And we'd have had to resurrect
one of them to find the criminal.'

'He won't be found, the criminal. He'll never be found,' the
Inspector said bitterly.

'But the pistol?' I asked. 'You had I believe some query
concerning the pistol . . . And it may well correspond to my
own.'

'What is it, your query?' Scalambri enquired condescend-
ingly.

'Simply this: why should the pistol, having vanished after
the first murder, be made available beside Don Gaetano's
body.'

'Correct,' said the Inspector. 'That's exactly what I say.'

152

'And what if it were someone else,' I said, 'who killed Don Gaetano? Someone who knew where the pistol was hidden or who happened to find it?'

'Oh God!' said Scalambri. 'Why complicate matters when they're quite complicated enough as it is? The pistol was hidden where the man who shot Michelozzi hid it — and hid it well. Nobody else could know where nor, whether by chance or by deduction, discover it. But if the Inspector thinks otherwise and admits that it was possible for someone else to find it he should acknowledge his own inadequacy and resign on the spot . . . Since it was his job to find it and for two days he hunted for it with a search warrant in every room, in every suitcase, inspecting every nook and cranny, covering every inch of ground.' Then pointing an accusing finger at the Inspector: 'Do you believe someone else found the pistol? That the man who murdered Don Gaetano wasn't the same who murdered Michelozzi?'

'I don't believe anything . . . I . . . But I just can't understand why the pistol was left there beside Don Gaetano.'

'Because it wasn't needed any longer. That might be why, mightn't it?'

'It might be,' said the Inspector. Simply to have done with it.

'And if it might be, why look for a more complicated and complicating answer?' Then turning to me: 'You know, when Don Gaetano was shot practically everybody was in his own room. And by "practically" I mean everyone except me, you, the Inspector, the policemen, the cook, the staff — and Don Gaetano. So that all the possible suspects were indoors, each in his room. At least that's what they all maintain and swear . . . The policeman on guard between the main staircase and the lift says that no one went out. Nor did he see anyone come in whom he hadn't seen leave. And the one on guard by the back stairs says the same thing. And the Inspector who was resting here on a deck-chair corroborates it — not a soul went out, not a soul came in . . . So what then?'

Obtaining no reply from us he answered his question himself — not without satisfaction: 'So then a reasonably simple solution presents itself, reasonably simple and reasonably sensible: one of the three, or two of the three, or all three abandoned their post for a minute — or more likely fell asleep.'

'Not me,' said the Inspector.

'All right. You neither abandoned your post nor fell asleep. Fine. And neither did the policeman on guard between the lift and the main staircase. But the one on guard by the back stairs . . . Look here, where exactly were you?'

'There,' the Inspector pointed.

'And from there can you swear that you were constantly watching the main entrance and the back entrance? Especially since you weren't there to keep watch but to have your siesta, to relax . . .'

'No. I can't swear.'

'There, you see? The policeman must have fallen asleep and you were looking the other way when the murderer stole out. There's no other explanation if we want to stay in the realm of logic, of common sense. Of course if we are prepared to abandon it we can reach any conclusion — we might even say that one of us three . . . You see, you say you were here having your siesta. But it's only you who say so . . . And you,' to me, 'you say you went . . . where exactly did you go . . . ?'

'To kill Don Gaetano,' I said.

'You see where it gets us, to abandon the path of common sense?' Scalambri said triumphantly. 'It gets us to the point where you, me, the Inspector are potential suspects just like those gentlemen, and more so. And without it being possible to ascribe to any of us a plausible reason, a plausible motive . . . I've always said it, my dear Inspector, always. The motive is what has to be found. The motive . . .'

They both remained silent for a few minutes. It had stopped raining; a ray of sunlight broke through the clouds. The carriage slowly jolted into Rome.

'In that case, I know what remains for me to do,' went on Anthime in his most decided voice. 'I shall give the whole show away.'

Julius started with horror.

'My dear friend, you terrify me. You'll get yourself excommunicated for a certainty.'

'By whom? If it's by a sham Pope, I don't care a damn!'

'And I who thought I should help you to extract some consolatory virtue out of this secret,' went on Julius, in dismay.

'You're joking! . . . And who knows but what Fleurissoire, when he gets to heaven, won't find after all that his Almighty isn't the real God either?'

'Come, come, my dear Anthime, you're rambling! As if there could be two! As if there could be another!'

'It's all very easy for you to talk — you, who have never in your life given anything for Him — you, who profit by everything — true or false. Oh! I've had enough! I want some fresh air!'

He leant out of the window, touched the driver on the shoulder with his walking-stick and stopped the carriage. Julius prepared to get out with him.

'No! Let me be! I know all that's necessary for my purpose. You can put the rest in a novel. As for me, I shall write to the Grand Master of the Order this very evening, and to-morrow I shall take up my scientific reviewing for the Depêche. Fine fun it'll be!'

'What!' said Julius, surprised to see that he was limping again. 'You're lame?'

'Yes, my rheumatism came back a few days ago.'

'Oh, I see! So that's at the bottom of it!' said Julius, as he sank back into the corner of the carriage, without looking after him.

André Gide, The Vatican Cellars

Also by Leonardo Sciascia and available from Granta Books
www.grantabooks.com

THE MORO AFFAIR

Extended edition with a new foreword

On 16 March 1978 Aldo Moro, a former Prime Minister of Italy, was ambushed in Rome. Within three minutes the gang killed all five members of his escort and bundled Moro into one of three getaway cars. An hour later the Red Brigades announced that Moro was in their hands; on March 18 they said he would be tried in a 'people's court of justice'. Seven weeks later Moro's body was discovered in the boot of a Renault parked in the crowded centre of Rome.

'The greatest compliment one can pay this fascinating book is to say that it reads like a fable about power anywhere in the world' *Independent*

'The Moro affair, the political crime, will not be forgotten; also, thanks to Sciascia, the tragic events have gained universal dimension. He has convinced us that real tragedies still happen, and that there is always further need of further criticism of our understanding and practice of power' *Irish Times*

SICILIAN UNCLES

A Sicilian uncle is a mentor, a patron, but a sinister and treacherous one. This quartet of novellas shows illusions being lost and ideals betrayed amid war and revolution. They are set at turning points of modern history: the revolutions of 1848; the Spanish Civil War; the Allied invasion of Sicily in 1943; and the death of Stalin ten years later. Each story is full of vivid characters and is like a door opening onto history.

'The best evocation of Sicily I've read, this is one for crime connoisseurs' Leslie Forbes, *Daily Mail*

'The master of sophisticated detective fiction remains Leonardo Sciascia, whose novels are an extended investigation into what it means to be Sicilian'
Guardian

'In ordinary detective stories there is always a good deal of disposable material, standard wrapping produced by the simple necessity of having things happen somewhere. There is nothing of the kind in Sciascia' Frank Kermode

EQUAL DANGER

District Attorney Varga is shot dead. Then Judge Sanza is killed. Then Judge Azar. Are these random murders, or part of a conspiracy? Inspector Rogas thinks he might know, but as soon as he makes progress he is transferred and encouraged to pin the crimes on the Left. But how committed are the cynical, fashionable, comfortable revolutionaries to revolution – or anything? Who is doing what to whom? This is one of Sciascia's best political thrillers.

'The master of sophisticated detective fiction' *Guardian*

'Only very rarely can we say of such works [crime novels]
that they look at questions of social justice with the
informed eye of the intelligent artist. We can, however,
make that claim for the stories of Leonardo Sciascia'
Frank Kermode

'The best evocation of the mafia in its birthplace in Sicily'
Evening Standard

THE DAY OF THE OWL

A dark-suited man is shot as he runs for a bus in the piazza of a small town. The investigating officer suspects the mafia, and soon finds himself up against a wall of silence and vested interests. As he uncovers a chain of nasty crimes, bystanders and watchers, complicit with secret power, gossip among themselves. Their furtive conversations have only one end: to stop the truth coming out.

This short novel about the mafia is also a mesmerising demonstration of how that organisation sustains itself. It is both a beautifully written story and a brave act of denunciation.

'One of the major writers of the age'
Times Literary Supplement

'Sciascia is so infuriatingly good that you wonder whether his Protean talents are not those of a secret syndicate'
Observer

THE WINE-DARK SEA

Here are some of Sciascia's greatest stories, brief and haunting: the realist tradition at its best.

In one tale a couple of men talk, cynically yet earnestly, about the etymology of the word 'mafia'. The reader comes to realise that he is eavesdropping on the musings of a mafia boss and his underling. In another story a group of peasants are taken on board ship and promised that they will be put ashore illegally at Trenton New Jersey. After a long time at sea, their landfall is far from what they expected. And Mussolini himself takes an interest in the case of Aleister Crowley, whose presence in Sicily has become embarrassing.

'Sciascia made out of his curious Sicilian experience
a literature that is not quite like anything else ever
done by a European' Gore Vidal